RAMAYANA REIMAGINED

THE ETERNAL LEGACY

PARTH D. JOSHI

Made with ♥ on the Notion Press Platform
www.notionpress.com

To my parents, my guiding light,
Who nurtured my dreams with endless might.

To my guru, Mahadev, divine and true,
Your blessings inspire all that I do.

To my grandparents, a treasure so rare,
For stories and wisdom beyond compare.

To my teachers, who shaped my way,
Your lessons still guide me every day.

To my dearest friend, steadfast and kind,
A bond eternal, heart and mind.

This work I offer, with love and grace,
To those who've filled my life's sacred space.

Contents

Preface

Ramayana Reimagined: The Eternal Legacy

The ancient epics in India are treasures that will never grow old. Time keeps giving them the stories and ideas. Among these, the great work of the Ramayana remains outstanding. It throws light on doing the right thing as a form of courage to be loyal and to stand out against some tough choices. Valmiki, a sage person, is the epic of this book; it has shaped how Indians think about right and wrong. But it's not just for India - people all over the world, in different times, have found meaning in it. Though many know the story well, there's still so much more to learn from it. We can look at it in new ways, think about what it means, and see how it fits with our world today. This is what "Ramayana Reimagined: The Eternal Legacy" aims to do. It brings back to life the stories of Rama, Sita, Lakshmana, Ravana, and many others. It shows how their wisdom could help us in understanding our lives now.

The Relevance of the Ramayana in Modern Life

As we delve into the pages of the Ramayana, we step into a world where divine intervention, human striving, and cosmic order converge in ways that resonate deeply with our current realities. Today, the world is riddled with challenges that test our resolve, character, and relationships. In this age of information, instant gratification, and ever-changing circumstances, the timeless lessons of the Ramayana are more relevant than ever before. They offer insights into human emotions, decision-making, moral struggles, and the eternal pursuit of dharma—the path of righteousness.

The Ramayana is not just an ancient story but a living philosophy that continues to guide the hearts and minds of individuals seeking answers to life's most profound questions. In these pages, the character of Rama exemplifies duty, integrity, and the ideal qualities of a leader, while his journey becomes a metaphor for the path of self-realization. Sita'sresilience and purity teach us about strength in adversity, while Lakshmana's unwavering loyalty highlights the value of devotion and support in relationships. Hanuman, the embodiment of courage and self-belief, reminds us of the transformative power of faith and the courage to face even the most daunting challenges.

For today's readers, the stories of the Ramayana offer more than just moral lessons; they provide a mirror reflecting our own struggles and triumphs. The dilemmas of love, loyalty, sacrifice, and identity portrayed in this epic continue to speak to the complexities of our modern existence. Whether we are dealing with difficult personal relationships, ethical decisions in the workplace, or the quest for meaning in a fast-paced world, the Ramayana offers answers grounded in values that are as relevant today as they were in ancient times.

A Storytelling Approach: Dadaji and Parth

What makes this reimagining of the Ramayana unique is the storytelling approach that bridges the ancient and modern worlds. The story unfolds through the conversations between a wise grandfather, Dadaji, and his curious grandson, Parth. This approach is designed to make the lessons of the Ramayana accessible, engaging, and meaningful for the modern reader. As Dadaji shares the great epic with his young grandson, each story not only captivates Parth's imagination but also sparks important reflections about life's values and challenges.

The choice of using a narrative between a grandfather and grandson is significant. Dadaji represents the wisdom of the ages—his experiences, insights, and values are passed down from one generation to the next. Parth, on the other hand, symbolizes the curiosity and inquisitiveness of the younger generation, seeking answers to questions that seem distant, yet are universal. The dialogues between them are more than just exchanges of stories; they are the moments where timeless wisdom meets the curiosity of a new world, creating a bridge between the past and the present.

Through this storytelling dynamic, the Ramayana comes alive in a way that is both traditional and contemporary. The complex themes of the Ramayana—such as dharma, loyalty, sacrifice, resilience, and the importance of duty—are explored in an accessible manner that can be appreciated by readers of all ages and backgrounds. The emotional and philosophical depth of the Ramayana is unpacked with the gentleness of a grandfather's wisdom and the eagerness of a child's questions.

Themes of Dharma, Sacrifice, and Resilience

One of the central themes of the Ramayana is the concept of **dharma**, the cosmic law that governs the universe and defines righteous behavior. Dharma is not a rigid set of rules but a flexible and dynamic principle that guides individuals through life's challenges. It speaks to the importance of acting in accordance with truth, justice, and virtue, while considering the greater good. Rama, the hero of the Ramayana, embodies this principle as he continually strives to live in alignment with his duty, even when it costs him personally. His decision to go into exile, his unwavering commitment to rescuing Sita, and his role as an ideal king—all reflect the pursuit of dharma.

In our modern world, the concept of dharma can be applied in myriad ways. It is about finding the balance between personal desires and societal responsibilities. It speaks to the importance of being true to one's word, upholding integrity in our actions, and ensuring that our choices contribute positively to the greater good. The lessons of dharma, as taught by Rama, can help guide us as we navigate the complexities of modern life, encouraging us to make decisions based on what is right, rather than what is easy.

The theme of **sacrifice** also runs deep through the Ramayana. Throughout the story, characters like Rama, Sita, Lakshmana, and even Ravana are forced to make sacrifices for their beliefs, loved ones, or kingdoms. Whether it is Rama's exile or Sita's suffering in captivity, sacrifice is portrayed as an integral part of the journey toward greater wisdom and self-realization. In a world where instant gratification is often prioritized, the Ramayana reminds us that true fulfillment often comes through sacrifices that contribute to personal growth and the welfare of others.

In the face of life's adversities, **resilience** is another quality emphasized by the Ramayana. The ability to endure hardship, to keep moving forward despite setbacks, and to emerge stronger through the trials of life is embodied in characters like Sita and Hanuman. Sita's strength in the face of Ravana's abduction and her unwavering faith in Rama teaches us the value of inner strength and hope. Hanuman's devotion to Rama, his bravery in crossing the ocean, and his determination to rescue Sita from Lanka reflect the transformative power of resilience in overcoming the most formidable challenges.

Characters as Modern-Day Archetypes

As we move through the Ramayana, we encounter a rich tapestry of characters who reflect different aspects of human nature. From Rama, the perfect man and ideal leader, to Ravana, the tragic villain undone by his own ego, the Ramayana offers a vast array of characters who each embody qualities that resonate with our own lives. By analyzing these characters, we can better understand our own tendencies, virtues, and flaws.

Rama, as the perfect leader, provides a model of leadership based on virtue, humility, and the pursuit of righteousness. His life is a testament to the importance of selflessness in leadership, of making decisions that benefit not just oneself but also the larger community. In the world of business, politics, and even personal relationships, the principles embodied by Rama offer valuable guidance for ethical leadership.

Sita's purity, strength, and devotion to Rama teach us about the importance of loyalty, integrity, and faith in one's values. Her story is one of enduring love, patience, and unwavering commitment. In relationships today, Sita's example reminds us of the importance of trust, honesty, and the power of inner strength to face challenges.

Lakshmana's unwavering loyalty to his brother, Rama, exemplifies the value of standing by those we love, no matter the cost. In our personal relationships and friendships, Lakshmana's character shows the power of support and sacrifice in building meaningful bonds.

Hanuman's courage, devotion, and self-belief encourage us to face our challenges with determination and faith in our own abilities. His devotion to Rama, combined with his remarkable feats, serves as a reminder that we all have the strength to overcome obstacles if we believe in ourselves.

Lastly, Ravana's downfall teaches us about the dangers of unchecked ego and pride. His story serves as a cautionary tale about the importance of humility and the consequences of allowing desires to overpower one's sense of duty and righteousness.

An Invitation to Explore

As you embark on this journey through the Ramayana Reimagined: The Eternal Legacy, we invite you to reflect on the timeless lessons offered by this ancient epic. Through the lens of Dadaji and Parth's conversations, you will not only experience the grandeur of this epic tale but also uncover the profound insights that can help navigate the complexities of modern life.

The Ramayana is not just a story of gods and demons; it is a narrative of human struggles, triumphs, and the constant search for truth. It is a story that transcends time and place, offering wisdom that can guide us through our personal journeys, no matter the era or circumstance.

May this book inspire you to delve deeper into the stories of the Ramayana, to reflect on its lessons, and to apply them in your own life as you walk the path of righteousness, courage, and love.

With heartfelt gratitude,

Parth D. Joshi

Acknowledgements

Writing this book has been an extraordinary journey—one filled with deep introspection, immense gratitude, and unwavering support from those who have been a part of my life. This book would not have been possible without the guidance, encouragement, and inspiration of many individuals, and I would like to express my heartfelt appreciation to each of them.

First and foremost, I am deeply grateful to my parents. Their love, sacrifices, and belief in my abilities have been the cornerstone of my journey. They instilled in me the values of hard work, humility, and perseverance, which form the very essence of this book. To my gurus, who imparted their knowledge selflessly, I owe my deepest respect and gratitude. It is through their teachings that I have learned the importance of discipline, dedication, and the pursuit of truth—values so vividly depicted in the Ramayana.

I offer my heartfelt devotion to Mahadev, my eternal guru, whose divine presence has been my guiding light. His blessings have provided me with clarity, strength, and the inspiration to pen this work. Every page of this book is a testament to the divine grace I have received throughout my life.

To my best friend, who has been my confidant, motivator, and constant supporter—I cannot thank you enough. Your encouragement, faith, and unwavering belief in my vision gave me the push I needed to begin and complete this journey. Your words of motivation in my moments of doubt were like a flame that never flickered.

I extend my gratitude to the timeless epic of the Ramayana itself, which has been my greatest source of inspiration. This ancient tale, composed by Sage Valmiki, remains an unparalleled guide to life, offering wisdom that transcends time and speaks to the human spirit. My humble attempt to present it in a new format would not have been possible without the divine brilliance of this sacred text.

To all the teachers and mentors in my life—those who shaped my mind and nurtured my ideas—I am forever indebted. Your wisdom and guidance have played a crucial role in bringing this book to life.

To my readers and well-wishers, you are the soul of this work. Your curiosity, questions, and desire to connect with our rich cultural heritage motivated me to write a version of the Ramayana that resonates with the modern world. This book was written for you, and I hope it brings you the same joy and enlightenment that I experienced while writing it.

I would also like to express my gratitude to my extended family and friends for their constant love and support. You have been my pillars of strength, reminding me that no journey is undertaken alone. To those who encouraged me to keep going, offered kind words, and showed patience during this process, I am profoundly grateful.

Finally, I must thank the divine universe for aligning all circumstances perfectly, allowing this book to come to fruition. It has been a journey of faith, dedication, and belief in something greater than oneself.

This book is not just my work—it is the result of collective love, guidance, and blessings from everyone who has been part of my life. I dedicate this book to all of you. May the wisdom of the Ramayana continue to illuminate our hearts, guide our choices, and inspire us to walk the path of righteousness.

With heartfelt gratitude,

Parth D. Joshi

Prologue

A Night Under the Banyan Tree

The air was cool, and the sky above the old ancestral home was speckled with stars. A gentle breeze rustled the ancient banyan tree in the courtyard, its sprawling roots reaching deep into the earth, much like the stories it had witnessed over centuries. On the wooden swing beneath its canopy sat Parth, an eight-year-old boy with a heart full of questions and a mind eager for stories. Beside him was his grandfather, Dadaji, a man whose wisdom seemed as vast and ageless as the tree under which they sat.

Parth's eyes sparkled with curiosity as he gazed at Dadaji. "Dadaji, why do we call Rama a hero? What made him so special?"

Dadaji leaned forward, his warm smile crinkling the corners of his eyes. "Ah, Parth, that's a question many have asked over thousands of years. Rama is not just a hero; he is an ideal. He embodies dharma—living righteously, even when life places obstacles in your path."

Parth tilted his head, intrigued. "Dharma? What does that mean?"

Dadaji chuckled softly, stroking his long, silver beard. "Dharma is like the guiding star in the sky, Parth. It's the path of truth and duty. For each person, it might mean something different, but it always leads to what is right. Rama's life is a lesson in how to follow dharma, no matter how hard the journey."

The boy leaned back on the swing, his young mind already racing with thoughts of this mysterious path. "Can you tell me his story, Dadaji? From the beginning?"

Dadaji's eyes twinkled as he gazed up at the starry sky. "Of course, Parth. But remember, this isn't just a story about a prince. It's about choices, sacrifices, and the fight between good and evil. To understand Rama's greatness, we must start from the very beginning—in a place called Ayodhya, the jewel of the Kosala kingdom."

Dadaji paused, letting the moment linger. The gentle rustle of the banyan leaves seemed to echo his words, as though the tree itself were preparing to bear witness to the tale.

"Long ago, Ayodhya was ruled by a noble king named Dasharatha," Dadaji began. "He was a man of great wisdom and kindness, loved by his people. But his heart carried a sorrow. Despite all his riches and power, he longed for a child, an heir to continue his lineage."

Parth's young face mirrored the emotions of the story. "Did he ever have children?" he asked eagerly.

"Ah, patience, my dear boy," Dadaji said with a wink. "All in good time. First, let's explore the magnificent kingdom of Ayodhya, a city like no other. It was a place of beauty, prosperity, and joy. But it was also where the seeds of an extraordinary journey were sown."

As Dadaji's voice wove the beginnings of the tale, the night deepened, and the stars above seemed to lean closer, as though they too wished to listen. Beneath the ancient banyan tree, the legacy of the Ramayana began to unfold once more, its timeless essence finding a new home in the heart of an eager young boy.

CHAPTER ONE

AYODHYA: A KINGDOM OF DREAMS

Introduction to the Kingdom of Ayodhya and its Prosperity

The setting sun cast a warm golden glow over the kingdom of Ayodhya, a city whose beauty seemed to rival the heavens themselves. The Sarayu River wound through the landscape like a silver ribbon, its gentle waves reflecting the shades of dusk. Tall trees stood in proud silence, their leaves swaying in harmony with the soft evening breeze. The temples, crafted from white marble, sparkled as the last light of the day kissed their domes. Majestic palaces, each a testament to the craftsmanship of the kingdom's artisans, dotted the landscape. In the courtyards, flowers bloomed in colors so vivid they could only be described as divine.

In this kingdom, prosperity flowed as effortlessly as the river itself. Trade from all corners of Bharat (India) brought wealth to Ayodhya, and its people were known for their hospitality, wisdom, and unwavering devotion to dharma. It was a city where truth and justice reigned supreme, and where every citizen, from the noble to the common, lived in peace. The kingdom's rulers had long been revered for their fairness and devotion to the welfare of the people. Among them was King Dasharatha, whose reign was marked by both wisdom and strength. He was a ruler beloved by all, known not only for his valor but for the kindness that filled his heart.

The people of Ayodhya held their king in the highest esteem, for his leadership brought them a life free from fear and want. Yet, in the midst of such prosperity, there was one thing that eluded him—the one thing that no wealth, power, or wisdom could provide: an heir. It was a yearning that weighed heavily upon his heart.

On this tranquil evening, as the scent of jasmine flowers filled the air, Dadaji looked at Parth and began his tale. "Ayodhya," he said softly, his voice carrying the weight of ages, "was a kingdom like no other. It was a land where dharma was upheld, where the gods themselves seemed to walk among mortals. The streets of Ayodhya hummed with joy, and its gardens were as vibrant as the souls of the people. The heart of this kingdom, Parth, was the royal family, the family that stood as the protector of dharma, a family that was about to face a test that would change their lives forever."

Dadaji's gaze grew distant, as if he could see the grand city in his mind's eye. "But even in such a kingdom, there was sorrow. A sorrow that filled the hearts of King Dasharatha and his queens, Kausalya, Kaikeyi, and Sumitra."

King Dasharatha's Yearning for an Heir

Parth listened intently as Dadaji's voice softened, carrying the weight of an emotion that transcended time.

"Dasharatha, the mighty king of Ayodhya, had everything—wealth, power, respect, and a prosperous kingdom. Yet, in the deepest corners of his heart, there was a yearning that could not be fulfilled. He had no children. No sons to carry his name. No one to sit on the throne after him. And in a kingdom where the continuation of the royal lineage was vital, this lack of an heir was a source of great sorrow."

Parth's eyes widened as he absorbed the depth of the king's sorrow. "But... how could he not have children, Dadaji? He was a king! Didn't he have everything?"

Dadaji smiled gently. "Ah, my dear Parth, that's the greatest lesson of all. Even the mightiest king, despite all his riches and grandeur, cannot command the one thing that truly matters—a child. A son to carry forward his legacy. You see, this was not just a personal longing for Dasharatha. It was the responsibility of a ruler to ensure that the kingdom remained in the hands of one who upheld dharma. Without an heir, the future of Ayodhya seemed uncertain."

Dadaji's voice took on a somber tone. "Despite all his power, Dasharatha could not bring a child into the world. He sought blessings from the wisest sages, performed rituals, and even gave offerings to the gods. Yet, no child was born to him. This sorrow weighed heavily on his heart. The king's once bright eyes became clouded with the longing for a son. He wondered: Would his name be forgotten? Would Ayodhya fall into darkness once he was gone?"

Parth sat quietly, imagining the king's pain. "But what did the king do, Dadaji? How did he find a way?"

The Putrakameshti Yagna and the Divine Arrival of Rama, Lakshmana, Bharata, and Shatrughna

Dadaji's expression shifted as he spoke of the moment that would change everything. "The king, in his desperation, called upon the gods themselves. He performed the Putrakameshti Yagna, a sacred and powerful ritual. It was not an ordinary ritual, Parth. This yagna was a call to the heavens. It was a plea for divine intervention. The fire was lit, and the prayers of the king rose up into the skies, carried by the smoke of sacred offerings."

"Dadaji," Parth asked, his curiosity piqued, "what exactly is a yagna?"

"A yagna is a fire ceremony," Dadaji explained patiently, "where offerings are made to the gods. It is a sacred ritual performed with the intention of bringing about a desired outcome. In Dasharatha's case, his desire was clear—a son, an heir. The yagna was performed with the utmost devotion, and it is said that the gods themselves were moved by Dasharatha's sincerity."

Dadaji's voice grew reverent as he continued. "As the flames of the yagna reached higher, something miraculous happened. From the fire emerged a divine being, a celestial figure who held in his hands a golden bowl filled with sweet, fragrant kheer. This kheer was no ordinary food, Parth. It was a gift from the gods themselves. The divine being instructed the king to give the kheer to his queens."

"The queens—Kausalya, Kaikeyi, and Sumitra—each partook of the kheer, and in that moment, the power of the gods filled their beings. It was not just nourishment; it was a blessing. A blessing that would soon bear fruit."

Parth's eyes sparkled with wonder. "So the queens ate the kheer... and then?"

Dadaji smiled warmly. "And then, Parth, the heavens smiled upon them. Each queen conceived a child, and in time, four sons were born to King Dasharatha. The eldest of these sons was Rama, a prince unlike any other, a child whose birth marked the beginning of a new era for Ayodhya."

Dadaji's voice became filled with pride. "Rama was born with the blessings of the gods, and his destiny was clear from the moment he opened his eyes. Alongside him were his brothers—Lakshmana, Bharata, and Shatrughna—each of whom was destined to play a role in the grand design of the universe."

Parth sat, his mind racing with the awe of what he had just heard. "So, these sons... they were chosen by the gods?"

Dadaji nodded slowly, his gaze distant. "Yes, Parth. These were no ordinary children. They were born of divine will, with a purpose far beyond the understanding of mere mortals. And from the moment they were born, Ayodhya rejoiced. It was not just the birth of sons, but the birth of hope itself. The kingdom had received its future, a future filled with righteousness, justice, and truth."

The Legacy of the Kingdom of Ayodhya

As the moonlight bathed the earth in its silver glow, Parth sat in silence, his mind brimming with questions. The weight of what he had just heard hung in the air, and the beauty of the kingdom of Ayodhya seemed to unfold before his very eyes.

Dadaji paused, allowing the weight of the moment to settle. "And so, Parth, the kingdom of Ayodhya, which had long yearned for an heir, had finally been blessed with not just one, but four sons. These sons would go on to change the course of history. Their story, Parth, is not just a tale of kings and princes. It is a story of dharma—of righteousness, sacrifice, and the unbreakable bond of family."

Parth's heart swelled with the sense of awe that only a story like this could bring. He looked up at Dadaji, eager to hear more. "What happens next, Dadaji?"

Dadaji's eyes twinkled with the kind of wisdom that only time could bestow. "Patience, my dear. The tale of Rama, his brothers, and the kingdom of Ayodhya is one for the ages. And as with all great stories, it will take you to places both wondrous and dark. But remember, every step they take is in the name of dharma, and it is a journey that will teach us all how to live, how to fight, and how to love."

CHAPTER TWO

THE MAKING OF A HERO: RAMA'S CHILDHOOD

Rama's Upbringing as an Exemplary Prince

The mornings in Ayodhya were bathed in golden light, and the palace, with its grand courtyards and lush gardens, echoed with the sounds of life. In the royal chambers, King Dasharatha would watch with pride as his four sons grew under the careful guidance of their tutors and sages. But it was the eldest, Rama, who stood out even at such a young age. His presence was regal, even in his playfulness. His face was serene, his heart pure, and his mind sharp—a combination that made him the ideal prince, worthy of the kingdom's legacy.

Dadaji's voice carried the weight of his wisdom as he began, "Rama, Parth, was no ordinary child. He was the very embodiment of dharma—righteousness, truth, and justice. Even as a boy, he was the perfect example of how a prince should be: brave, wise, compassionate, and just. He would often be found playing with his brothers, but even in games, he displayed qualities that would later define him as a leader—fairness, honor, and a sense of responsibility."

Parth imagined a young Rama—his chest puffed with pride as he held his bow, his brothers laughing beside him. "Rama was not like other boys, Parth. His heart was always attuned to the needs of others. He knew, even then, that his purpose was far beyond the confines of a palace."

Dadaji paused, his voice growing more reflective. "Every morning, King Dasharatha would call upon the royal teachers to guide his sons in the ways of archery, politics, and warfare. But above all, he wanted to ensure that his sons were well-versed in the art of dharma. His greatest desire was that they would lead the kingdom with wisdom, and in that, he placed his trust not only in his advisors but also in the ancient teachings of the sages."

The Training of the Four Brothers Under Sage Vishwamitra

One day, as the sun reached its zenith, a visitor came to Ayodhya—an esteemed sage who was known throughout Bharat for his wisdom and unparalleled power. His name was Vishwamitra, and he had come not just as a traveler but with a purpose. He had heard of the four royal sons, and it was with great anticipation that he sought an audience with King Dasharatha.

Dadaji's voice grew stronger as he spoke of the arrival of Sage Vishwamitra. "Vishwamitra was no ordinary sage, Parth. His strength was not just in his mind but also in his spirit. He had the power to command the elements, to summon celestial beings, and to protect the righteous. But despite all his power, he had one great desire—he wanted to train the sons of Dasharatha. He had seen the spark of greatness in Rama, and he knew that these boys would play a role in the world's destiny."

When the sage arrived at the royal court, King Dasharatha welcomed him with great reverence. But as the sage spoke of his intentions, the king's face clouded with worry. "Vishwamitra, you seek to take my sons with you?" he asked, his voice tinged with concern. "They are young, and their place is here, with their people."

But Vishwamitra's gaze was unwavering. "It is true that they are young, Dasharatha. But there is a fire in these boys that cannot be extinguished by the comforts of the palace. They must be tested, trained in the ways of war and dharma. If you wish for them to be true rulers, you must send them on a path that will forge their souls."

Dadaji's eyes gleamed as he spoke of what followed. "And so, it was decided. The four brothers—Rama, Lakshmana, Bharata, and Shatrughna—set off on a journey that would change them forever. The path was treacherous, filled with dangers and trials, but it was also a path that would make them legends."

The brothers, under the guidance of Vishwamitra, traveled to the dense forests of the north. The air there was thick with mystery, and the wild creatures roamed freely. The sage, known for his immense power, guided them with both wisdom and discipline. Day after day, they practiced archery, swordsmanship, and the ancient techniques of warfare. The brothers were quick learners, but it was Rama who showed an extraordinary prowess. He could aim his bow with such precision that even the mightiest of foes would tremble at the thought of facing him.

Parth's eyes sparkled with curiosity. "What kind of training did they undergo, Dadaji? What did they learn?"

Dadaji smiled, his voice softening as he described the lessons. "The lessons of dharma were as important as the lessons of war. They were taught to honor truth, to respect the gods, and to always protect the weak. But the most important lesson, Parth, was in the art of controlling one's mind. The mind is the greatest weapon a warrior can possess. To wield it properly is to be invincible."

As the days passed, the brothers became masters in their own right. Lakshmana, ever devoted to Rama, learned to fight with unmatched speed and precision. Bharata, with his strong sense of duty, excelled in strategy and leadership. And Shatrughna, the youngest, displayed a keen understanding of tactics and perseverance.

The Thrilling Defeat of Rakshasas Like Tataka and Subahu

The training, however, was not to be without its tests. One day, as the brothers and Sage Vishwamitra trekked deeper into the forest, they encountered a danger that would challenge their strength, courage, and resolve. The forest, known for its beauty, was also home to dark creatures—rakshasas, demons who thrived on terror and chaos.

Sage Vishwamitra led them to a clearing, where the air was thick with an unsettling silence. "This is the forest of Tataka," he warned. "It is a place where only the brave dare tread. And here, you will face your first true test."

At that moment, a deafening roar split the silence. From the shadows emerged a towering demoness, her form twisted and monstrous. Her name was Tataka, and she had terrorized the forest for years. Her eyes glowed with malice, and her very presence sent chills down the spine of anyone who dared to enter her domain.

"Rama," Vishwamitra called, his voice steady. "You must defeat her."

Without hesitation, Rama nocked an arrow to his bow, his face calm, his eyes unwavering. He pulled the string back, and with a swift release, the arrow shot through the air like lightning. The demoness screamed as the arrow struck her, and in an instant, she fell to the ground, vanquished. The forest was quiet again, the danger subdued.

Parth sat wide-eyed, astonished by the scene. "Did Rama really defeat her with just one arrow, Dadaji?"

Dadaji nodded. "Yes, Parth. Rama's mastery over his bow was unmatched. But what made his victory even more remarkable was that he did not act out of anger or revenge. He acted out of dharma, to protect the innocent from harm. Tataka's death was necessary for the peace of the land."

But the dangers did not end there. As they continued their journey, they encountered Subahu, another rakshasa who had allied himself with Tataka. He stood before them, armed with dark magic and malice in his heart.

"This time," Vishwamitra said, "it will not be as easy. But I trust you, Rama."

Rama, with unwavering resolve, prepared for battle. The sky darkened as the rakshasa conjured a storm, hurling lightning and fire at the brothers. Yet Rama remained calm, his focus sharp. With a mighty roar, he released another arrow, this one infused with divine power. The arrow tore through the air, striking Subahu and reducing him to ash.

Dadaji's voice grew heavy with the weight of the moment. "In that moment, Parth, Rama proved not just his strength but his unwavering commitment to dharma. He did not seek glory, but simply the restoration of peace."

The brothers returned to Ayodhya after their training, each stronger and wiser. They were not just princes anymore. They were warriors forged by trials, by the teachings of Sage Vishwamitra, and by their own hearts. They had learned that true strength comes not from the power of the body but from the purity of the soul.

Parth, sitting beside Dadaji under the banyan tree, reflected on what he had heard. "Rama... he was destined for greatness, wasn't he, Dadaji?"

Dadaji smiled, his eyes twinkling with the wisdom of ages. "Yes, Parth. He was destined for greatness. But greatness is not something that is given. It is something that is earned, through courage, righteousness, and the will to protect those who cannot protect themselves. And this, my dear, is just the beginning of Rama's journey."

CHAPTER THREE

THE BOW THAT CHANGED DESTINY

The Journey to Mithila

The sun had begun its descent, casting golden rays across the land, as the great city of Ayodhya buzzed with excitement. Today was not just another day; it was a day that would change the course of destiny. Prince Rama, along with his brothers, had just received the news that had set the royal household in motion: the famous swayamvara of Sita, the princess of Mithila, was soon to take place.

Dadaji's voice, rich with warmth and depth, filled the quiet evening air. "Rama, Lakshmana, Bharata, and Shatrughna were eager to undertake this journey to Mithila. But for Rama, this was not just about winning a bride. It was a journey that carried the weight of dharma, of fate itself. They traveled through dense forests, crossed rivers, and braved treacherous terrains, all the while keeping their focus on the prize—Sita, a woman of unparalleled virtue, beauty, and wisdom."

Parth, sitting cross-legged on the floor beneath the banyan tree, his eyes wide with curiosity, asked, "What was so special about Sita, Dadaji? Why was the whole kingdom in a frenzy?"

Dadaji paused for a moment, his gaze drifting into the distance as if recalling a distant time. "Sita was no ordinary princess, Parth.

She was the embodiment of purity, of dharma. She had been born from the earth itself, a blessing from Mother Bhumi. Her beauty and grace were matched only by her intelligence and kindness. The swayamvara, a contest where a princess chooses her husband from a group of suitors, was to be held at Mithila, where she had been raised under the guidance of the wise King Janaka."

As the story unfolded, Dadaji's words transported them to the grand city of Mithila, where preparations for the swayamvara were in full swing. The royal palace stood tall, adorned with flowers and banners, and the air was thick with excitement. Kings, princes, and noblemen from far and wide had gathered to witness the event, each hoping to win the heart of the divine princess.

The Grand Swayamvara

Mithila's palace was a sight to behold, with its grand halls and intricate carvings that told the stories of the ancient gods. Dadaji's voice echoed the grandeur. "The swayamvara was to be held in the great hall of Mithila, where the most powerful and revered kings were invited to test their strength and skill. The contest was centered around a mighty bow—the Bow of Shiva—said to be the strongest weapon known to the gods. The challenge was simple: the prince who could string the bow and lift it would win Sita's hand in marriage."

Parth's eyes narrowed with interest. "But why would the bow be so important, Dadaji? What was special about it?"

Dadaji smiled, his voice rich with wisdom. "The Bow of Shiva was no mere weapon. It symbolized the unbreakable strength of dharma. No ordinary man could wield it, and no weak-hearted prince could even lift it. It was said that only a person with the purest intentions and unmatched strength could succeed in this task. For Sita, the bow was a test not just of physical power but of worthiness. Only a prince who was true to dharma, who respected righteousness above all else, could win her heart."

As Dadaji spoke, the scene in Parth's mind came alive. Rama and his brothers had arrived at the gates of Mithila, where the entire kingdom had gathered to witness the swayamvara. The crowd, filled with anticipation, looked upon Rama with admiration and respect. His presence alone was enough to captivate everyone, his princely demeanor and quiet confidence setting him apart from the rest.

The Suspenseful Breaking of Shiva's Bow

When the time came, the mighty bow of Shiva was placed before the assembly. It was no ordinary weapon; it was enormous, made of a dark, heavy wood that seemed to hum with an ancient power. The other princes, eager to prove their strength, stepped forward one by one, each attempting to lift the bow. Some tried with all their might, their muscles straining, but none could even budge it.

Parth was leaning in, clearly intrigued by the unfolding events. "Did none of them succeed, Dadaji?"

"None," Dadaji replied softly, his voice taking on a tone of reverence. "The bow was a symbol of divine strength, and only one destined to wield it could succeed."

Rama stepped forward with quiet grace. As he approached the bow, a hushed silence fell over the crowd. There was a sense of awe in the air. Rama, calm and composed, took hold of the bow with both hands. His movements were deliberate, not rushed, as though he understood the weight of the moment. He placed one knee on the ground, gripped the bow firmly, and with a single fluid motion, he bent it. The bow, which had withstood the strength of many great warriors, cracked under his touch. The sound reverberated through the palace, the noise of the breaking bow echoing like thunder.

The crowd was stunned into silence. In that moment, it became clear: Rama was no ordinary prince. His strength, his character, and his worthiness were beyond measure. With one simple action, he had not only completed the challenge but had also proven that he was the one destined to be Sita's husband.

Parth could hardly contain his excitement. "Did he win, Dadaji? Was Sita's heart his?"

Dadaji smiled warmly. "Indeed, Parth. In that moment, Rama not only won the bow but also won the heart of Sita, who was watching from the balcony. But remember, this was not just a contest of strength. It was a contest of values. Rama's humility, his purity of heart, and his respect for dharma shone brighter than any bow ever could."

The Wedding of Rama and Sita

The court erupted in applause, and Sita, her heart filled with admiration for the prince, descended from her palace. The wedding preparations began almost immediately. It was a moment of pure joy, but beneath the celebration, there was a deep sense of respect and reverence for the union that was about to take place. This was not just a marriage; it was the coming together of dharma and purity, the union of two souls destined to fulfill a higher purpose.

Sita, dressed in the finest silks and adorned with jewels that shimmered like the stars, stood before Rama. Her eyes, filled with both awe and love, met his. And in that gaze, an unspoken promise was made—a promise of loyalty, sacrifice, and unwavering commitment to dharma.

The priest, his voice booming with divine authority, began the sacred rites. The fire, the symbol of truth and purification, blazed before them as they exchanged vows. "With this fire as witness," the priest chanted, "may your hearts remain united, may your lives be filled with righteousness, and may your love for one another remain as pure as the flame before you."

The wedding was not just a union of two people; it was a union of ideals, of purpose. Rama and Sita's bond symbolized the very essence of dharma—truth, virtue, and duty. As they circled the sacred fire, the onlookers could sense that something much deeper than a simple marriage was unfolding.

Dadaji's voice softened, his words heavy with meaning. "Rama and Sita's wedding was not just a joining of two lives, Parth. It was a divine coming together, a bond that would withstand every trial, every challenge, for they were destined to walk a path of righteousness together."

Parth sat back, absorbed in the gravity of the tale. "And they lived happily ever after, Dadaji?"

Dadaji smiled, a knowing look in his eyes. "Ah, Parth, their story is far from that simple. But remember this: their love was the foundation of all that came after. The challenges they faced, the sacrifices they made—each one was a testament to the purity and strength of their union. It was a love rooted in dharma, and that is what made it eternal."

In the silence that followed, the evening seemed to pause, as if the very earth around them held its breath. The tale of Rama and Sita's wedding had unfolded like a delicate flower, and in that moment, Parth understood that their story was not just a myth, but a guiding light for all who sought to walk the path of dharma.

And so, under the ancient banyan tree, Dadaji's voice continued to weave the tale of Rama, Sita, and the eternal legacy of their love.

CHAPTER FOUR

A Mother's Betrayal: Kaikeyi's Boons

The Courtly Intrigue

The peaceful rhythm of Ayodhya was about to be shattered. The kingdom that had once flourished under King Dasharatha's wise reign now stood at the precipice of a great upheaval. It began with whispers, unnoticed by the court at first, but they soon grew louder. The royal palace, which had once been a haven of joy, became a stage for a courtly intrigue that would alter the course of history.

Dadaji leaned forward, his voice heavy with the weight of the tale. "King Dasharatha had long been a beloved ruler, and his kingdom prospered under his rule. But even the wisest of kings is not immune to the twists of fate. His three queens—Kausalya, Sumitra, and Kaikeyi—were the pillars of the royal family, each holding a special place in the king's heart. Yet, it was Kaikeyi, his youngest queen, who would soon make a demand that would shake the very foundations of their world."

Parth listened intently, sensing the shift in Dadaji's tone. "But Dadaji, what could Kaikeyi want? She had everything—wealth, power, and the love of her husband."

Dadaji sighed, his eyes clouding with sorrow. "Yes, Parth, she had everything. But desire is a powerful force, one that can cloud even the most pure of hearts. Kaikeyi had once saved King Dasharatha's life in battle, and in gratitude, the king had promised her two boons. These boons, once meant to be a gesture of kindness, would soon become the weapons that would shatter the peace of Ayodhya."

The scene shifted in Parth's mind as Dadaji's words painted the picture of a kingdom on the edge of turmoil. Kaikeyi, once the cherished queen, had grown ambitious, and her heart was now ruled by jealousy and fear. She knew that the time had come for her son, Bharata, to ascend the throne. But for that to happen, Rama—Dasharatha's beloved eldest son—would have to be removed from the throne.

Kaikeyi Demands Her Boons

It was a bright morning when Kaikeyi, with a serene yet determined expression, entered the royal court. The courtiers and noblemen stood at attention, their eyes following the queen as she made her way to the throne. King Dasharatha sat at his regal seat, his heart filled with pride as he watched his sons—Rama, Lakshmana, Bharata, and Shatrughna—prepare for the coronation ceremony of Rama. The kingdom was to rejoice as its future king was to be crowned, and the air was filled with anticipation.

But as Kaikeyi approached the throne, an unease settled over the room, and the jubilant atmosphere began to shift. There was a coldness in her eyes, a sharpness in her gaze that spoke of a deep resolve.

"Dasharatha," Kaikeyi began, her voice calm but filled with an undeniable authority, "I have come to claim my two boons, which you once promised me in gratitude for saving your life."

Dasharatha, momentarily taken aback, smiled warmly at his queen. "Of course, Kaikeyi. I remember the promise well. Ask, and it shall be granted. Whatever you wish, my dear, is yours."

But there was no joy in Kaikeyi's eyes now, only a fierce determination. She stepped closer, her next words cutting through the air like a dagger. "I ask for two things, O King. First, that your beloved son Rama be sent into exile for fourteen years. And second, that my son, Bharata, be crowned the king in his place."

The words struck Dasharatha like a thunderclap, the echo reverberating through his very soul. The court fell into stunned silence. It was as though time itself had frozen in place. How could Kaikeyi—his once loving and devoted queen—demand such a thing? He searched her face, hoping to find a hint of jest, but there was none. Her eyes were cold, her expression unreadable.

"Kaikeyi," King Dasharatha whispered, his voice trembling with disbelief. "You ask for Rama's exile and Bharata's coronation? What has caused this sudden change in your heart?"

But Kaikeyi remained unmoved. "It is not sudden, my Lord. I have watched Rama's growing influence, his growing closeness to the throne, and I have seen the power he holds in the hearts of the people. Bharata deserves to be the ruler of Ayodhya, and he will be, with your blessing."

The shock of the moment left Dasharatha speechless. His entire world seemed to tilt on its axis, and he could hardly comprehend what Kaikeyi was asking of him. His gaze flickered to Rama, who stood in the court, his face a picture of grace and composure. Rama, whose heart was filled with love for his father, could not have imagined such a betrayal from his own stepmother.

The Emotional Turmoil

The moment the decree was made, the kingdom of Ayodhya plunged into a storm of emotions. The very air seemed heavy with grief and disbelief. Dadaji's voice quivered as he recalled the emotional turmoil that gripped the royal family. "Rama, who had always been obedient to his father, was heartbroken. He could not fathom why Kaikeyi, who had once been like a second mother to him, would ask for such an injustice. His love for his father, his sense of duty, and his unwavering devotion to dharma were tested as never before."

Parth's brow furrowed. "But Dadaji, why did King Dasharatha agree to Kaikeyi's demand? Wasn't he the king? Didn't he have the power to refuse?"

Dadaji nodded slowly, his eyes sad. "Yes, Dasharatha was a king, but he was also a father, a man bound by his promises and his word. Kaikeyi had threatened him with the loss of his honor, and in the moment of her demand, he felt powerless to do anything but comply. The love he had for his sons, particularly Rama, clouded his judgment, and he felt helpless in the face of Kaikeyi's manipulation."

As the news of Rama's exile spread throughout the palace, a deep sadness fell upon the family. Sita, Rama's wife, could not bear the thought of being separated from him. She was a woman of unwavering loyalty, and the idea of Rama leaving for fourteen years filled her heart with dread. But her love for him was so profound that she made a decision that would shape the course of their lives.

Rama, Lakshmana, and Sita stood together in the royal court, preparing to leave. The three of them, bound by love and duty, knew that their lives would never be the same again. Lakshmana, ever the loyal brother, insisted on accompanying Rama into exile, vowing to remain by his side no matter the hardships they might face. Sita, despite the great pain in her heart, decided to follow her husband into the wilderness, for she could not bear to live without him.

"Do not worry, Dadaji," Parth said quietly. "They will face the trials together. I know they will."

Dadaji smiled softly. "Indeed, Parth. Their bond was unbreakable, and they would walk the path of exile together, facing whatever came their way. But it is in moments like these that the true strength of one's character is tested. Rama, with his calm demeanor and unwavering commitment to dharma, would soon face challenges that would test not only his strength but his very soul."

As the family stood in the palace, the moment of separation drew near. King Dasharatha, torn by sorrow and regret, could not bear to look upon Rama, who stood before him, composed and dignified. "Rama, my son," Dasharatha whispered, his voice breaking. "I have failed you, and I can never undo the pain I have caused you. Forgive me, my son, for I have broken my heart as well as yours."

Rama, his heart heavy yet filled with love for his father, knelt before him. "Father, your words do not wound me. I understand your duty. I will go into exile, as you have commanded, with the same respect I have always shown you. For I know that this is the path of dharma."

The moment was one of profound emotion, and as Parth listened to the tale, he felt a deep sense of awe at the strength of character Rama displayed in the face of such adversity. "Rama truly is a hero, Dadaji," Parth said softly. "His ability to forgive and remain steadfast in his duty is beyond words."

Dadaji nodded, his voice filled with admiration. "Indeed, Parth. Rama's heart was pure, and his commitment to dharma was unshakable. This was the trial of exile, the beginning of his journey into the wilderness. And it would be a journey that would test every part of his soul."

The trial of exile had begun, and in the silent forests of the world, where only the whispers of the wind and the rustling of the leaves could be heard, Rama, Sita, and Lakshmana would walk their path. It was a path of sacrifice, of duty, and of a love that would endure through the greatest of trials.

WANDERING HEARTS: INTO THE FOREST

The Journey Begins

The sun had barely risen when Rama, Sita, and Lakshmana set forth from the gates of Ayodhya, their faces etched with both resolve and sorrow. The weight of their departure pressed down on their hearts, but their steps were firm, for they knew the road ahead would be long and fraught with challenges. King Dasharatha, his heart breaking, had been unable to stop them, despite his deep sorrow and regret. With each step, the walls of the palace and the city faded behind them, and the vast, untamed wilderness stretched out before them, a new world that awaited their arrival.

Dadaji's voice was soft as he continued the tale. "As they left the city, the very air seemed to change. Gone were the sounds of the bustling kingdom, the chatter of the market, and the joyous laughter of the people. Instead, the silence of the forest welcomed them—a silence both eerie and peaceful. It was as though the trees themselves whispered ancient secrets, as if the earth was holding its breath, watching the royal family take their first steps into exile."

Parth, his mind adrift, felt the weight of that silence in his chest. "What was it like, Dadaji? To leave everything behind?"

Dadaji smiled softly, his eyes clouded with the memory. "It was a moment of profound change, Parth. The forest was no longer just a place—it was now their home, their sanctuary, and their trial. As they walked deeper into the wilderness, the familiar comforts of royal life seemed like distant dreams, replaced by the simple yet harsh realities of survival."

The path ahead was uncertain, but the trio moved forward with a grace that seemed to come from their very souls. The grandeur of their royal attire faded into the simplicity of their new lives as exiles. Their regal demeanor remained, but their hearts had already begun to embrace the solitude and challenges of the wilderness.

The Enchanting Forests

The forests that surrounded them were thick with towering trees, their canopies heavy with foliage that blocked out the sun, casting the path below in dappled shadows. The earth beneath their feet was soft with layers of fallen leaves, and the air was rich with the scent of damp soil and the sweet fragrance of wildflowers. It was a world that was both beautiful and wild—untouched by the hands of man, yet teeming with life in every corner.

"Imagine, Parth," Dadaji said, as he began describing the landscape, "a forest so vast that it seemed to stretch into infinity. The trees were ancient, their trunks thick and gnarled, their branches twisting high into the sky like the arms of the earth reaching toward the heavens. The wind rustled through the leaves, carrying with it the songs of unseen birds and the whispers of the forest itself."

As they journeyed deeper into the forest, the trio encountered a multitude of creatures. From the rustling of small animals in the underbrush to the distant call of wild beasts, the sounds of the forest were ever-present. The air, thick with the earthy scent of the woods, was alive with energy, each rustle of the trees seeming to speak in a language older than time itself.

"Look, Dadaji," Parth exclaimed, his eyes wide with wonder. "What about the animals and creatures in the forest? Did Rama and his companions meet them?"

Dadaji chuckled, nodding. "Indeed, they did. The forest was home to all manner of creatures, some benevolent and others less so. But Rama, ever kind and compassionate, treated every living being with respect. It was in the heart of this wilderness that the true test of their character began. They learned to live as one with the forest, its challenges, and its blessings."

Their journey took them through dense thickets, across sparkling streams, and up winding mountain paths. In the heart of the forest, the trio found not only solace but also a deep connection to the world around them. The forest was no longer just a place they were passing through—it had become a living, breathing entity, a silent guide on their journey.

Encounters with Sages

As they traveled deeper into the forest, they encountered many sages and hermits who had long made their homes in the wilderness. These sages were known for their wisdom and their deep connection to the divine, living lives of seclusion and meditation, away from the distractions of the world.

Dadaji's voice grew more reverent as he recounted the first of these encounters. "One such sage they met was the venerable Valmiki, the very sage who would later pen the epic tale of Rama's life. Valmiki, who lived by the banks of the river Tungabhadra, welcomed Rama and his companions with great warmth and respect. His hermitage was a place of peace, where the air was thick with the scent of incense and the sound of flowing water. The sage saw in Rama the embodiment of dharma—the very essence of righteousness—and he knew that the prince was destined for greatness."

Parth's eyes widened in amazement. "So, Valmiki knew even then that Rama's story would become legendary?"

"Yes, Parth," Dadaji continued, his voice filled with awe. "Valmiki had a divine vision of Rama's future, and he could see that the trials and challenges that lay ahead for the prince would shape him into the greatest hero the world would ever know. The sage, knowing the importance of Rama's journey, offered his blessings, praying for his success and safety."

Rama, in his usual humble and respectful manner, bowed before the sage. "I am honored to meet you, wise one," he said. "Please bless me on this journey, for I walk not only for myself but for the sake of my dharma and my people."

Valmiki's eyes shone with a divine light as he placed his hands on Rama's head. "May your journey be fruitful, O Rama," he said, his voice imbued with a quiet power. "May you be steadfast in your devotion to dharma and may your heart always remain pure. The forest may be your home for now, but remember that your true kingdom lies in the hearts of those who follow the path of righteousness."

Rama, ever grateful, thanked the sage and continued on his way. "We shall continue on, Valmiki, with your blessings to guide us."

As they traveled further, the trio encountered other sages, each of whom offered them counsel and blessings for their journey. The sage Agastya, a revered hermit known for his wisdom, greeted them with kindness and shared valuable knowledge about the dangers of the forest. He spoke of the rakshasas who roamed the wilds, of the trials they might face, and of the need for vigilance in the face of evil.

"Be strong, Rama," Agastya said, his voice carrying the weight of centuries. "The forest is not without its dangers, but your heart is pure, and you are protected by the divine. The rakshasas may try to tempt you, but remember that your strength lies in your unwavering devotion to dharma."

As Agastya finished his words, he presented Rama with a bow—a weapon of great power, crafted by the gods themselves. "This bow,"

Agastya said, "is a gift to aid you in the trials ahead. It is a weapon of justice, and it shall serve you in your time of need."

Rama accepted the bow with gratitude, his heart heavy with the responsibility that came with it. "Thank you, sage. Your blessings and this weapon shall guide us through the trials ahead."

The Spirit of the Forest

As Rama, Sita, and Lakshmana ventured deeper into the forest, the wilderness seemed to embrace them as one of its own. They slept beneath the stars, their dreams filled with visions of the challenges they would face. The days turned into weeks, and the weeks into months, but the bond between the trio grew stronger with each passing day.

The forest was no longer a place of exile but a home—a sanctuary where they found strength not only in each other but in the world around them. The bond between them, forged in love and duty, became the very foundation of their journey. And as the years passed, their lives in the forest became a testament to the power of dharma, of unwavering devotion, and of the unbreakable spirit of those who walk the path of righteousness.

Dadaji's voice softened as he finished the story. "And so, Parth, Rama, Sita, and Lakshmana found peace in the wilderness. They lived simply, but their hearts were full. They had left behind the comforts of the palace, but in the forest, they found a deeper connection to the world and to themselves."

Parth, his mind filled with images of the vast forests and the wise sages, nodded thoughtfully. "It's amazing, Dadaji, how their journey wasn't just about the trials they faced, but about how they grew stronger in spirit."

Dadaji smiled, his eyes twinkling. "Indeed, Parth. And this was just the beginning of their journey. The trials they would face in the forest would be the foundation of their destiny, and they would learn much about themselves, about the world, and about the power of dharma."

As the tale came to a close, the winds outside seemed to carry a faint whisper—a reminder of the vast, untamed world that awaited the trio, where every step would be a step closer to their destiny.

26

CHAPTER SIX

SHADOWS OF THE DARK: THE RAKSHASAS' WRATH

A Peaceful Yet Perilous Life

For many days after leaving the familiarity of Ayodhya, Rama, Sita, and Lakshmana lived peacefully in the dense, whispering forests of Dandaka. The forest stretched endlessly before them, its mysteries unfolding in the serenity of nature. Their daily life consisted of simple routines—gathering food, performing rituals, and enjoying the purity of the wilderness. Sita, ever graceful, would spend her days gathering flowers and offering prayers, while Lakshmana, ever vigilant, kept a sharp watch over their surroundings. Rama, in his quiet strength, meditated on the path of dharma, constantly learning from the forest's stillness.

But even in the most serene of places, shadows can lurk. The forest of Dandaka, though seemingly peaceful, was known for its darker side—the rakshasas, demon-like creatures who roamed the wilderness, feeding off its isolation. Though Rama's exile brought him to this sanctuary, it also placed him in the path of these malevolent beings. It was inevitable that their lives would be disturbed by these sinister forces.

Dadaji's voice took on a mysterious tone as he continued, drawing Parth into the narrative. "The rakshasas, Parth, were not ordinary creatures. They were evil beings who thrived in the wilderness, and their very presence caused suffering to the sages and hermits who sought peace in the forest. They were cruel, cunning, and relentless, and wherever they went, they spread chaos."

Parth sat forward, eager to hear more. "So, what happened when Rama and his companions met these rakshasas?"

Dadaji smiled knowingly, his eyes twinkling with the thrill of the story. "Ah, this is where the true test of Rama's character begins. One day, while Rama, Sita, and Lakshmana were spending their days in the forest, a rakshasi named Surpanakha appeared. She was no ordinary demoness—her beauty was both captivating and deadly. She wandered into their peaceful abode with the intention of sowing discord, and her actions set the stage for an unrelenting chain of events that would change everything."

The Encounter with Surpanakha

Surpanakha was a rakshasi, the sister of Ravana, the mighty king of Lanka. She had heard of Rama's princely charm and strength, and she came to the forest seeking to captivate him. Her heart burned with lust for the prince, her mind consumed with thoughts of him. When she saw Rama from afar, his radiant presence under the green canopy of the forest, she was struck by his divinity and grace. At that moment, she desired him fiercely, believing that he, too, would be captivated by her beauty.

Surpanakha approached Rama with a seductive smile, but her intentions were far from pure. "O handsome prince, your beauty rivals the very gods. Come, join me in my kingdom. There is no greater pleasure than to be with me," she declared, her voice a mixture of sweet temptation and cold malice.

Rama, ever wise and composed, regarded her with the calm detachment of someone who had seen the world's illusions for what they were. "I am already bound by my dharma and my vows to my wife, Sita," Rama replied gently. "I have no place for desires beyond my duties."

At this, Surpanakha's face contorted with rage. Humiliated and enraged by Rama's rejection, she turned to Sita, whose beauty surpassed even her own. Her jealousy turned to venom. "You dare refuse me, Rama? I shall destroy the very one you love most."

In an attempt to carry out her wicked plan, Surpanakha lunged toward Sita with a cruel grin. But Lakshmana, always protective of his brother and his beloved Sita, was quicker. In a flash, he drew his sword and severed Surpanakha's nose and ears, leaving her disfigured and humiliated. The once-beautiful rakshasi fled into the forest, vowing revenge on Rama and his family.

The Revenge of Ravana

Surpanakha, humiliated and enraged, returned to her brother Ravana in Lanka. Her face was a twisted mask of fury, and her heart seethed with a thirst for vengeance. She told Ravana of Rama's rejection, of how he had disfigured her, and of Sita's unparalleled beauty.

As Ravana listened to his sister's tale, his heart burned with anger and lust. He was a powerful and fearsome king, but something in Surpanakha's words stirred something deep within him. The beauty of Sita, combined with the humiliation his sister had suffered, ignited a desire for revenge and an obsession that would soon bring the wrath of the demon king upon the entire world.

Dadaji paused for a moment, his voice grave as he continued, "Ravana, though a mighty king, was a man consumed by arrogance and desire. He could not stand to be mocked, especially by a mere mortal like Rama. Surpanakha's injury became a deep wound to his pride. His heart, already steeped in darkness, now sought to wreak havoc upon Rama's life."

Ravana sent his trusted ally, the powerful golden deer, Maricha, to the forest in disguise, hoping to lure Rama away from his family with the illusion of a beautiful creature. The demoness' rage and Ravana's growing obsession were about to lead to the most perilous part of the journey for Rama, Sita, and Lakshmana. This would be a turning point, one that would set the stage for a series of fateful events that would alter the course of their lives forever.

Maricha's Deception

One quiet afternoon in the forest, Rama and Lakshmana were training, while Sita rested beneath the shade of a tree. The tranquility of the forest was disturbed by a most enchanting sight. A golden deer appeared in the distance, its fur gleaming like the sun itself. Sita, ever captivated by beauty, gazed in awe at the majestic creature. She turned to Rama, her voice soft with longing, "O Rama, please capture this golden deer for me. It is so beautiful, and I wish to have it as a companion."

Rama, sensing that something was amiss, looked closely at the deer, his instincts tingling with caution. "It is no ordinary deer, Sita," he said slowly, his gaze fixed on the creature. "But if it pleases you, I will try to capture it."

He told Lakshmana to guard Sita and stay behind as he ventured deeper into the forest after the golden deer. Lakshmana, reluctant to let his brother go alone, hesitated. "But brother, this is no ordinary beast. It is likely a trap laid by the rakshasas."

Rama smiled gently, his voice steady. "Do not worry, Lakshmana. I will return soon. You must guard Sita. Stay strong, and remember that dharma is our guiding force."

Lakshmana nodded reluctantly, and Rama pursued the golden deer, his bow drawn and his eyes sharp. As he chased the creature through the dense forest, the deer seemed to elude him at every turn. Finally, when Rama had cornered it, the creature turned to face him, and in that moment, its true form revealed itself: it was none other than Maricha, the rakshasa in disguise.

With a deep, mournful cry, Maricha called out, "Rama, please, do not harm me! I am merely a pawn in Ravana's scheme."

But it was too late. Rama, with unshakable resolve, shot an arrow that pierced the rakshasa's chest. Maricha fell to the ground, his cries echoing through the forest.

The Crisis at the Cottage

Back at the cottage, Sita heard Maricha's cries echoing through the trees. The sound was chilling, and her heart filled with dread. She turned to Lakshmana, her eyes wide with concern. "Lakshmana, something is wrong. Please go to my husband. I fear for his safety."

Lakshmana, ever devoted, hesitated, sensing the potential danger of leaving Sita alone. But Sita's distress was undeniable, and he reluctantly set off to find Rama.

Just then, a figure appeared on the horizon—a tall, powerful figure, cloaked in shadow. It was Ravana.

The Kidnapping of Sita

Ravana, with his dark, supernatural power, approached the cottage in the guise of a wandering sage. His voice was smooth and deceptive, "O noble lady, you are alone in the forest. I come in peace, seeking alms. Please offer me your hospitality."

Sita, ever compassionate, rose to greet him, unaware of the danger that lurked beneath the sage-like exterior. As she stepped forward, Ravana seized the moment. With one swift motion, he snatched her up and, in the blink of an eye, flew off with her in his chariot, bound for Lanka.

Sita cried out for Rama, her voice filled with terror and desperation. But no one was near to hear her cries. The forest fell silent once again, as the evil forces of Ravana began to tighten their grip on the world.

Dadaji paused as the room grew heavy with the weight of the story. "And so, Parth, with Sita's abduction, the true battle between good and evil was set in motion. The forest, once a place of refuge, had now become the backdrop for a war that would shake the heavens themselves."

Parth, his heart racing, leaned forward. "What happened next, Dadaji? How did Rama react?"

Dadaji's gaze turned somber. "That, Parth, is where the true test of Rama's strength and dharma begins."

CHAPTER SEVEN

The Illusion of Gold: The Enchanted Deer

The Enchanting Appearance of the Golden Deer

It was a serene day in the forest, where the gentle rustling of leaves and the distant calls of birds created a harmonious symphony. Rama, Sita, and Lakshmana, ever at peace in their simple life, had set up a humble dwelling beneath the shade of towering trees. The air was rich with the earthy scent of moss, and the sunlight filtered softly through the canopy above, casting dappled shadows on the forest floor.

Sita, dressed in simple yet elegant attire, sat in quiet contemplation as she gazed out at the natural beauty around her. She had grown accustomed to the forest's solitude, and its tranquility had become her sanctuary. Yet, beneath the serenity, there was an underlying feeling of longing that often stirred in her heart.

One day, while resting, Sita's eyes were drawn to something unlike anything she had ever seen before. A creature appeared in the distance, its fur gleaming with a golden sheen, as if the very sun had decided to take form. The golden deer moved gracefully through the trees, its movements ethereal, almost otherworldly. It was so beautiful that it seemed to have stepped out of a dream.

Sita's breath caught in her throat. She turned to Rama, who was sitting nearby, lost in thought. Her voice, soft with wonder, broke the peaceful silence. "Rama, look! See that golden deer! It is unlike anything I've ever seen before. Please, capture it for me. It would be the most beautiful gift I could ever have in this wilderness."

Rama looked at the deer, his sharp eyes scanning the creature with his usual cautious nature. He could feel something amiss, something not quite right about the deer. Yet, he knew how much it meant to Sita, and her request, though seemingly simple, carried the weight of her heart. He turned to her with a gentle smile.

"Sita, this is no ordinary deer. Its beauty is captivating, but I sense that it is not what it seems. However, if it pleases you, I will try to capture it."

Sita's eyes sparkled with excitement. "Oh, Rama! Please! I would be so happy if you could bring it to me. It would be a treasure."

Without another word, Rama stood and readied himself to pursue the creature. Lakshmana, ever the protector, looked at his brother with concern.

"Rama, be careful. There is something strange about this deer. It may be a trap laid by the rakshasas."

Rama's expression softened as he reassured Lakshmana. "Do not worry, Lakshmana. I will return soon. Watch over Sita, and stay strong."

With that, Rama took off into the forest, his figure blending with the shadows as he pursued the elusive golden deer.

The Illusion Unfolds

As Rama ventured deeper into the forest, he found himself mesmerized by the graceful movements of the deer. It darted through the trees, and no matter how fast he ran, it stayed just out of reach. The chase became a thrilling pursuit, and for a moment,

Rama forgot the warning in his heart. He was entirely absorbed in the hunt, determined to fulfillSita's wish.

The golden deer, however, was no ordinary creature. As Rama followed it deeper into the forest, it led him farther and farther away from his wife and brother, until the peaceful sounds of the forest gave way to an eerie silence. The trees seemed to close in around him, the air grew thick, and the distant sounds of the forest faded into nothingness.

Finally, after what seemed like an eternity, Rama caught up to the deer. In that moment, the creature stopped and turned toward him. But as Rama notched an arrow and aimed for the kill, the golden deer revealed its true form. With a dreadful screech, the creature transformed into Maricha, the rakshasa who had been sent by Ravana to deceive him.

Maricha, now in his rakshasa form, lay dying on the forest floor, his once beautiful body now grotesque and monstrous. With his last breath, he cried out, "Rama, it is I, Maricha, in disguise. I was sent by Ravana, your enemy, to lead you astray. Beware, for the danger that awaits you is far worse than you know."

Rama, heart heavy with realization, rushed to Maricha's side. The demon had deceived him with the illusion of the golden deer, a cunning trap laid by Ravana. But as Maricha's voice faded into the forest, Rama's heart was gripped with an ominous foreboding.

Before he could fully grasp the weight of the danger, Maricha's final cry echoed through the trees. "Sita... Sita is in danger..."

The Cry for Help

Back at the cottage, Sita sat anxiously, her heart filled with unease. The sight of the golden deer had been enchanting, and now that Rama had pursued it, she was left alone with her thoughts. The silence seemed to stretch for too long, and with each passing minute, her worry grew.

Suddenly, from the depths of the forest, a cry pierced the air—a desperate, heart-wrenching call for help.

"Sita! Sita!"

The voice, unmistakable, was that of Rama. It carried with it a sense of urgency, of peril. Sita's heart pounded in her chest as she jumped to her feet, her eyes wide with alarm. But something was wrong. It was not the calm, steady voice of her husband. There was a strange desperation in his cry, a tremor of fear that she had never heard before.

At that moment, she turned to Lakshmana, her voice trembling with concern. "Lakshmana, please, something is wrong. I fear for Rama. You must go to him at once. His call was filled with danger. Please, do not delay."

Lakshmana, ever loyal and protective, looked at his brother's wife, sensing the weight of her distress. But deep down, he knew there was a reason why Rama had asked him to remain behind. He could not leave her alone in the forest.

"Sita, I cannot leave you alone," Lakshmana said firmly, trying to calm her. "I must stay and protect you. You are my responsibility, just as Rama is."

Sita's distress grew, her voice growing more urgent. "But Lakshmana, Rama needs help! Please! He is calling for me!"

Her plea echoed in the stillness of the forest, and the truth of the situation weighed heavily on Lakshmana's heart. After a moment of silent deliberation, he reluctantly agreed to go. "Stay inside the cottage, Sita. I will not be long."

With that, he hurried off into the forest, determined to find Rama and bring him back to safety.

The Deceptive Sage

As Lakshmana disappeared into the trees, the silence returned to the cottage. The air was thick with tension, and Sita, though comforted by Lakshmana's promise, could not shake the growing fear in her heart.

It was then that a figure appeared on the horizon. A tall, regal man approached the cottage, his gait steady and composed. His appearance was that of a wandering sage, draped in simple robes, his face serene and calm. But there was something unnatural about the figure. Something in the way he moved that sent a chill down Sita's spine.

He came closer, and in a smooth, soft voice, he called out to her, "O noble lady, you are alone in the forest. I am but a humble sage, seeking alms. Please, show kindness to an old soul."

Sita, ever compassionate, stepped forward to greet him, her heart heavy with the weight of her growing anxiety. "I am sorry, sage, but I cannot offer you anything. I am alone, and my husband is not here. Please, you must understand."

The sage's face remained impassive, but his eyes gleamed with a hidden, malicious intent. "Ah, but you are not alone, Sita. Your husband is far away, and it is only right that I, too, share in the fruits of your charity."

Before Sita could react, the figure revealed his true form: it was Ravana, the demon king of Lanka, disguised as a sage. With terrifying strength, he seized Sita and carried her away in his chariot, leaving behind the safety of the forest and plunging the world into chaos.

Sita's Captivity

As Sita was taken away, the world seemed to stand still. Her cries for help echoed into the wilderness, but no one could hear her. The earth beneath her seemed to tremble as she was carried away by Ravana, her heart heavy with fear and uncertainty.

Dadaji's voice grew quieter, his gaze far away as he continued the story. "And so, Parth, this was the beginning of the greatest trial of Rama's life. Sita, whom he loved dearly, had been taken from him. The peaceful forest, where they had once lived in bliss, had now become a battleground between good and evil. And from this moment forward, nothing would ever be the same again."

Parth, feeling the weight of the moment, asked, "What happened next, Dadaji? How did Rama find Sita?"

Dadaji's voice was firm as he continued, "Rama, Parth, would stop at nothing to rescue his beloved Sita. The path ahead was fraught with danger, but his resolve was unshakable. The journey for justice had only just begun."

CHAPTER EIGHT

THE DEMON'S DISGUISE: RAVANA'S DECEPTION

The Arrival of the Deceptive Mendicant

The serene air of the forest had already been disturbed by the unsettling events of the day, and now, a new shadow loomed over the tranquil dwelling of Rama, Sita, and Lakshmana. Sita, her mind still burdened with the uncertainty of Rama's absence, stood at the entrance of their humble hut, gazing longingly into the dense forest. Her heart ached with the memory of Rama's call for help, still ringing in her ears.

But as she stood there, trying to soothe her anxious heart, a figure appeared at the edge of the clearing—a figure so calm, so serene, that it could only be a sage, a wandering mendicant who sought alms. His appearance was plain, almost ordinary, yet there was something about him that seemed to exude a strange aura of power, despite his simple attire. He approached her, his steps slow and deliberate.

Sita, always compassionate, felt a sense of calm as she gazed upon him. It was not uncommon for wandering ascetics to pass through the forest in search of alms, and though she had never seen this one before, she was familiar with the ways of the world.

"Dear lady, I am a humble sage, wandering in search of charity," the figure said, his voice smooth and gentle, carrying the calmness of a thousand years. His voice was not loud, but it seemed to reverberate in the still air of the forest, drawing Sita's attention as if it were a spell.

Sita, feeling the need to offer assistance, stepped forward, her eyes soft with kindness. "I have nothing to offer you, sage, except what little I can spare. My husband, Rama, is far away in pursuit of a golden deer, and my brother-in-law, Lakshmana, has gone to his aid. Please, if you require anything, I shall offer what I have."

The mendicant smiled, his lips curling into an expression of practiced sweetness. "Ah, Sita. You are the epitome of compassion, a true daughter of the Earth. But I ask for nothing from you, except for your kindness in hearing me out."

With each word, the figure's presence seemed to grow stronger. His calm demeanor made Sita'ssuspicions fade, and in the momentary lull, she allowed him to speak further.

The mendicant's eyes glinted mischievously. "Sita, you are known far and wide as the epitome of virtue, but there is a greater purpose that awaits you. You shall soon join your true destiny."

Before Sita could respond, the mendicant began to change. His form shimmered like a mirage, his simple robes transforming into royal garb, his once gentle face now twisting into a sinister mask. Sita's eyes widened in horror as she realized, with a shock to her very soul, that the mendicant before her was none other than Ravana, the demon king of Lanka.

In that instant, Ravana seized Sita, his powerful hands closing around her delicate form. Sita's breath caught in her throat as she screamed for help, but the words died in the air, swallowed by the vastness of the forest. Before she could react, Ravana lifted her effortlessly into the air, and in the blink of an eye, she was pulled away from her home, her world, her safety.

The PushpakaVimana: A Chariot of Death

As Ravana's colossal form lifted Sita into the sky, the forest beneath her grew smaller and smaller, until it was but a mere speck in the distance. The vastness of the world seemed to stretch infinitely before her. She fought against his hold, but Ravana's grip was unyielding, and soon, she was bound by invisible forces, unable to escape.

Ravana's chariot, the **PushpakaVimana**, a magnificent aerial vehicle borne by the wind, loomed before them. The Vimana was unlike any chariot she had ever seen—vast, resplendent, and luminous, it seemed to defy the laws of nature. Its golden frame gleamed as if it were forged from the sun itself, its wings vast and majestic, reminiscent of the birds of the sky that soared in ancient myth.

The PushpakaVimana floated high above the earth, its majestic structure adorned with gemstones that glittered like stars in the night sky. The chariot's wheels, though still, seemed to spin in the air, casting an eerie glow as they sailed through the vast expanse. The air around the Vimana shimmered with an unnatural energy, and the winds carried with them a strange, unsettling hum.

As Sita gazed out from the confines of the Vimana, her heart filled with terror. Below her, the earth seemed to grow smaller, the land of Ayodhya receding far beyond her reach. She had no idea where Ravana was taking her, but she knew that her life had been changed forever. The feeling of helplessness gripped her heart, for she knew that her husband, Rama, would stop at nothing to rescue her.

Despite her fear, Sita's heart clung to the memory of Rama's strength, his love, and his promise to protect her at all costs. She closed her eyes for a moment, praying to the gods for help, for guidance, and for the strength to endure the perilous journey ahead.

Ravana, ever the cunning demon, spoke in a voice full of pride, his words dripping with malice. "Sita, you are destined to be mine. No one will save you now. Your husband, Rama, is weak. Even if he comes after you, he will never be able to defeat me. Lanka will be your new home, and I shall make you my queen."

Sita's heart swelled with defiance. "I am already promised to Rama. You will never have me. I would rather die than belong to one such as you."

Ravana's laugh echoed through the skies, dark and menacing. "We shall see, Sita. We shall see."

The Journey to Lanka

As the **PushpakaVimana** soared through the clouds, Sita's thoughts turned to Rama. She could not help but remember their love, their bond, and the promise he had made to her when they had first met. She could not believe that this moment had come—Ravana had taken her from her home, from the safety of her family, and from the one person she loved more than anything.

Yet, in the deepest corners of her heart, she held onto hope. She knew that Rama was not a man who would simply give up. He was a warrior, a hero, and above all, a protector. His resolve would not falter, even in the face of overwhelming odds.

The journey to Lanka stretched on, but Sita's spirit remained unbroken. Her prayers and thoughts were with Rama as the **PushpakaVimana** carried her farther and farther away from the land she knew, into the heart of enemy territory. No matter what Ravana did, she would not lose hope. She would endure. Rama would come for her. The thought was her guiding light in the darkest of times.

Dadaji paused in his narration, his voice growing soft and steady. "And so, Parth, Sita, the beloved wife of Rama, was carried away to the distant lands of Lanka, bound by Ravana'sdark magic. The road ahead was fraught with danger, but for Sita, as for Rama, the battle had only just begun. Their fates were intertwined, and no force in the world could break their bond."

Parth, listening intently, asked in a hushed voice, "What happened after that, Dadaji? How did Rama find Sita?"

Dadaji's voice grew firm as he continued, "The story of Rama's quest to find his beloved Sita is a tale of unwavering determination, courage, and righteousness. Rama's journey had just begun, and he would stop at nothing to rescue his wife from the clutches of Ravana."

And so, the story of Rama and Sita continued, with each twist and turn drawing them closer to the epic confrontation that would change the course of history forever.

CHAPTER NINE

WHISPERS OF HOPE: THE SEARCH FOR SITA

The Grief of Rama and Lakshmana

The tranquility of the forest was shattered, and an uneasy silence replaced the lively sounds of nature that had once accompanied Rama, Sita, and Lakshmana in their exile. The sun had set on what should have been an ordinary day in their secluded forest home. But as Rama returned from the pursuit of the golden deer, he was met with a desolate and heart-wrenching sight—his beloved Sita was gone.

The silence hung heavily in the air, as if the earth itself mourned. Rama's heart, ever filled with courage and resolve, now felt a cold, gnawing emptiness. His eyes darted around their humble abode, as if hoping to see Sita emerge from behind the trees, her radiant smile greeting him. But there was nothing. No sound. No sign of her.

The absence of Sita was not just the loss of a wife—it was the breaking of a bond so sacred, so deeply intertwined with his very soul, that it felt as though a part of him had been ripped away. The forest, which had once seemed like a haven, now seemed alien and unforgiving. The thought of the terrible uncertainty that lay ahead gripped him, and in that moment, Rama knew that nothing would ever be the same again.

He called out, his voice carrying through the trees, but there was no response.

"Lakshmana!" Rama's voice was hoarse with a mixture of shock and rising panic. "Where is Sita? Where has she gone?"

Lakshmana, ever the faithful brother, appeared at his side in an instant. His heart raced as he too took in the absence of their beloved sister-in-law. Though he too shared in the deep anguish that filled the air, he knew that there was no time to waste. The search for Sita would begin immediately.

"Rama," Lakshmana said softly, placing a hand on his elder brother's shoulder. "We will find her. We must. She is somewhere in this world, and we will search every inch until we bring her back."

But Rama, his brow furrowed in frustration and anguish, looked out into the forest, as if searching for answers that were beyond him. "But where? How could this happen? She was right here, in this very place."

Lakshmana's voice remained steady as he spoke the unspoken truth: "The only one who could have taken her is Ravana. We must not waste any more time."

Together, the brothers stood in the shadow of their now-ruined world. The wilderness stretched out before them like a dark, endless maze. Each step they took, each breath they drew, felt like a journey into an unknown void—a void that had taken their beloved Sita.

The Encounter with Jatayu

As Rama and Lakshmana ventured deeper into the forest, the weight of their sorrow was palpable. The trees seemed to grow taller, the shadows deeper, as if the very land shared in their grief. Yet amidst the desolation, a faint glimmer of hope flickered in their hearts. They knew they could not afford to surrender to despair. Their duty was clear, their mission defined.

Days passed with little to no sign of Sita. The forest, which had once seemed so familiar, now seemed full of dangers, each more threatening than the last. The brothers searched tirelessly, calling out for Sita, but their calls were swallowed by the vastness of the wilderness.

It was on one of these endless days, as they walked in silence, that they first saw the aged vulture—Jatayu—circling above them. The bird seemed to be flying low, its wings casting a shadow over the brothers as they gazed upward, drawn by its presence.

Rama's eyes widened. "That is Jatayu, the noble vulture who is known far and wide for his strength and wisdom."

Lakshmana nodded, his heart filled with hope. "If anyone knows where Sita is, it is Jatayu."

The brothers quickened their pace and soon stood before the great bird, who was perched on a rocky outcrop. Jatayu, though old and frail, still possessed an air of majesty and power that made him a revered figure in the forest.

"Jatayu!" Rama called out, his voice filled with urgency. "Have you seen my wife, Sita? A demon named Ravana has taken her. Please, tell us what you know."

Jatayu, his wings rustling gently, lowered his head to meet Rama's gaze. His eyes, though dimmed with age, still held a glimmer of strength and wisdom.

"Rama," Jatayu said in a voice raspy from years of flight, "I saw it all. Ravana, the demon king of Lanka, took your wife from the forest. I tried to stop him, but I am old, and he is powerful."

Rama's heart clenched with pain at the mention of Sita's abduction. His breath caught in his chest as he struggled to suppress the wave of anguish that threatened to overwhelm him.

"Where did Ravana go?" Lakshmana asked, his voice filled with determination.

Jatayu's voice grew faint, as if the memory of the moment itself had drained his strength. "Ravana took her toward the south, in the direction of Lanka. I fought him with all my strength, but he was too powerful. Before he took flight, he struck me down. Yet, I know where he went. It is to Lanka, where he rules."

Rama's eyes narrowed with grim resolve. "Thank you, Jatayu. Your bravery will not be forgotten. You have given us the knowledge we need."

As Jatayu spoke, his voice grew weaker, his body frailer. He had given all he had to warn Rama and Lakshmana, and now the vulture, in his final moments, seemed ready to pass on.

"Rama," Jatayu said softly, his voice barely a whisper, "I may not live to see your triumph, but I know you will rescue your wife. I am at peace, knowing that I have done all I could."

With those final words, Jatayu closed his eyes, and his lifeless form slumped forward. Rama and Lakshmana stood in silence, their hearts heavy with both sorrow and gratitude.

"Rest in peace, noble Jatayu," Rama whispered, bowing his head in reverence. "You have given us the strength to continue."

The Path Forward

With Jatayu's final words guiding them, Rama and Lakshmana knew they could no longer afford to hesitate. Lanka was now their destination, and they would stop at nothing to reclaim Sita from the clutches of Ravana.

As they journeyed southward, the forest began to change, its once familiar trees growing denser, the air thick with the scent of unfamiliar plants. Yet there was no turning back. Every step they took seemed to echo with the memory of Jatayu's sacrifice and the hope that Sita was still alive.

Rama's heart burned with a singular purpose. He had already faced numerous trials on his journey, but this—this was the most important. He would not fail her. No matter what it took, no matter the price, he would bring Sita back.

And so, with the memory of Jatayu guiding their path, Rama and Lakshmana set forth toward the distant land of Lanka, where the fate of Sita and the kingdom of Ayodhya would be decided.

As Dadaji spoke softly, his voice filled with the weight of the moment, "And so, Parth, the search for Sita began in earnest. With the knowledge of her abduction and the guidance of Jatayu, Rama and Lakshmana embarked on the most important journey of their lives. The path ahead was fraught with dangers, but nothing would deter them from their mission. Nothing would stop them from rescuing Sita."

Parth, eyes wide with wonder, asked, "Dadaji, do you think they will find Sita?"

Dadaji's eyes sparkled with a quiet confidence. "Rama's determination is unwavering, Parth. The story of his devotion to Sita is a tale that has inspired generations. And no matter how dark the path may seem, there is always light at the end."

And so, the tale of Rama and Sita continued—full of peril, hope, and undying love.

A Friend for Eternity: Meeting Hanuman

The Arrival at Kishkindha

Rama and Lakshmana had traveled far from the tranquil forests of Panchavati, where their lives had once been marked by the simplicity and serenity of exile. Their journey now led them to the rugged, wild landscapes of Kishkindha, a kingdom nestled in the heart of the dense forests. Kishkindha was a land of great beauty but also untamed wilderness, known for its formidable rulers and its connection to the mighty vanaras—monkey-like warriors who roamed the vast stretches of forest.

Kishkindha, however, was not just a land of beauty; it was also a kingdom teetering on the brink of its own fate. For months now, it had been locked in internal strife. The vanara king, Vali, and his brother Sugriva had been bitter enemies, their conflict disrupting the peace of the entire region. The kingdom, once prosperous, now lay fractured by sibling rivalry.

Rama and Lakshmana, however, had no time to become entangled in the politics of Kishkindha. They had only one purpose in mind: to find Sita. After the tragic loss of Jatayu, who had passed away while trying to protect her from Ravana's abduction, their hope rested on finding new allies, and the vanaras of Kishkindha, it seemed, could provide that assistance.

As they entered the borders of Kishkindha, they were greeted by the dense foliage and towering trees that stretched far beyond the horizon. There was a sense of something ancient and wise in the air—a feeling that this land, though full of untamed forces, had witnessed many great deeds.

Rama and Lakshmana walked together, their determination unshaken despite the overwhelming weight of their mission. They had no knowledge of what awaited them in Kishkindha, but the journey had left them no choice but to trust that allies would emerge to help them in their most desperate hour.

The Encounter with Sugriva

The brothers wandered through the vast forest of Kishkindha, searching for signs of the vanara king Sugriva. Their quest was urgent, for the kingdom of Lanka seemed farther away with each passing day, and they could not afford to waste time.

It was during these moments of uncertainty that a figure appeared on the distant horizon. This figure, large and imposing, seemed to stride through the forest as if the very earth respected his presence. This was no ordinary creature. With a mighty leap, the figure landed before Rama and Lakshmana with the power of an avalanche.

Sugriva, the exiled king of Kishkindha, stood before them, his stature awe-inspiring. He was a vanara of great strength, his body muscular and his face adorned with the battle-hardened features of a king in exile. His eyes, however, were filled with a deep sorrow—a reflection of the turmoil he had faced in his own kingdom.

"I am Sugriva, the son of Surya," he introduced himself with a voice that resonated in the air, the sound of a leader who had seen much and endured even more. "I have heard of your plight, O noble

Rama. The news of Sita's abduction has reached even these distant forests."

Rama's heart swelled with a mixture of relief and hope. At last, an ally had appeared who might aid them in their search for Sita.

"I am Rama, son of Dasharatha, and this is my brother, Lakshmana," Rama replied, bowing his head in respect. "We are in search of my wife, Sita, who has been taken by Ravana, the demon king of Lanka. We seek your help, O mighty Sugriva. We have heard of your strength and valor. Will you aid us in our quest?"

Sugriva's eyes glistened with both grief and resolve. His own heart ached with the knowledge that his kingdom had been torn apart by his brother, Vali, and that he had been exiled for reasons beyond his control. However, the plight of Rama stirred something deep within him—an empathy and a recognition that, just like him, Rama too had faced an unjust exile and loss.

"I am in your debt, noble Rama," Sugriva said, stepping closer. "I shall lend you my strength and my army of vanaras. But first, there are matters to be settled in Kishkindha. For I am not yet free from the grip of my brother, Vali, who rules this kingdom with an iron fist."

Hanuman's Introduction

As Sugriva spoke of his exile and his ongoing battle with his brother, Vali, Rama and Lakshmana listened intently. But amidst Sugriva's words, a new figure appeared in the clearing. This figure moved with such grace and swiftness that the brothers scarcely had time to react.

This was Hanuman, the son of the wind god Vayu. His arrival was like the gust of a mighty storm—an overwhelming presence that seemed to fill the very air around him. Hanuman was unlike any other creature they had encountered. His body was as powerful as it was agile, his eyes gleaming with intelligence and strength. A warrior of immense power, yet his demeanor was humble, radiating a quiet wisdom that immediately commanded respect.

"Rama," Sugriva said, turning to face the newcomer. "This is Hanuman, the most loyal and powerful of my vanara warriors. There is no one in Kishkindha more capable than he. If anyone can aid you in your quest, it is Hanuman."

Rama's gaze shifted to Hanuman, and a deep sense of reverence filled his heart. Here stood a being of incredible strength, and yet there was an aura of humility that surrounded him, as though he was not swayed by his power.

Hanuman bowed respectfully before Rama and Lakshmana. His voice was deep yet filled with warmth. "O noble Rama, son of King Dasharatha, I have heard of your virtues and your noble cause. I, Hanuman, am at your service. Wherever you go, I shall follow. Whatever you ask, I shall do."

Rama, moved by Hanuman's words, smiled with gratitude. "Hanuman, I am honored to have you by my side. You are as mighty as the wind itself, and your heart is filled with devotion. With your strength and loyalty, we shall find Sita and defeat the forces of evil that stand in our way."

The Bond Between Rama and Hanuman

Hanuman's eyes gleamed with determination as he spoke. "Rama, my strength is yours, and my soul is devoted to you. Together, we shall achieve victory."

And so, a bond was forged between Rama and Hanuman—one that would prove unbreakable, transcending the boundaries of loyalty, strength, and devotion. Hanuman, the son of the wind god, now stood beside Rama as a trusted ally. His heart, filled with the power of the divine, would guide Rama in ways that no one else could.

The story of Hanuman, the devoted servant of Lord Rama, would soon unfold in its entirety, but this meeting marked the beginning of a powerful alliance—one that would change the course of the epic forever.

Rama, looking at Hanuman with a sense of trust and gratitude, spoke softly, "Hanuman, you are not just my ally. You are my friend, and you shall always have a place by my side."

And as the sun began to set over the dense forest of Kishkindha, the three of them—Rama, Lakshmana, and Hanuman—sat together, their hearts bound by a shared mission and a common purpose: to rescue Sita and restore righteousness to the world.

Dadaji paused as he recalled this moment, his voice rich with the weight of the words, "Parth, this meeting with Hanuman was the turning point in Rama's journey. It was not just about finding Sita; it was about gathering the strength to face what lay ahead. Hanuman was more than a warrior—he was the embodiment of loyalty, courage, and devotion. And from that day forward, no force in the world could stand in the way of Rama's mission."

Parth, wide-eyed, asked eagerly, "Dadaji, what happened next? How did Hanuman help Rama?"

Dadaji smiled knowingly. "Ah, Parth, Hanuman's true power had yet to be revealed. But what he would do for Rama in the days to come would go beyond anything you could ever imagine..."

And with that, the story of Rama, Lakshmana, and Hanuman continued, as they began their preparation for the epic battle that lay ahead.

ACROSS THE OCEAN: HANUMAN'S LEAP OF FAITH

The Quest for Lanka

Rama, Lakshmana, and Hanuman had forged a bond that seemed unbreakable. Together, with Sugriva'svanara army now behind them, they were ready to begin the most critical part of their journey—the search for Sita. The path ahead was fraught with challenges, but their determination was unmatched. The journey to Lanka was not only a geographical one but also a trial of their courage, resilience, and faith in each other.

Their first obstacle was the vast ocean that separated them from Ravana's kingdom, a seemingly insurmountable barrier that stretched out as far as the eye could see. The ocean, with its treacherous waters and powerful currents, was a formidable force, mocking their every step.

Rama, who had always shown profound wisdom and patience, turned to his allies. "The ocean is vast and unyielding," he said thoughtfully. "We need a way to cross it and reach Lanka. Only then can we confront Ravana and free Sita from his clutches."

As the vanaras mulled over possible solutions, Hanuman—always the one to think outside the box—stepped forward. His powerful, fearless nature had earned him the trust of Rama, and in this moment, his resolve was even stronger. Hanuman had always been a symbol of unwavering devotion and strength, but now his true test was about to begin.

Hanuman's Leap Across the Ocean

"Rama," Hanuman spoke with complete confidence, "I will leap across the ocean and find a way into Lanka. Once I reach Ravana's kingdom, I will discover where Sita is held, and return with news of her whereabouts."

Rama, looking at Hanuman with a mixture of pride and gratitude, nodded. "Hanuman, you have shown yourself to be the embodiment of courage and loyalty. I trust in your strength and your determination. Go forth, my friend, and bring us news of Sita."

The vanaras, too, watched with awe as Hanuman prepared for what would be one of the most epic feats in the history of the Ramayana. His strength, boundless as the winds, would now be put to the ultimate test. With a deep breath and a look of unshakable resolve, Hanuman positioned himself at the edge of the shoreline.

With one final glance at Rama and his brothers, Hanuman closed his eyes and began to chant a prayer to his father, the wind god Vayu, who had blessed him with the strength and ability to perform such a miraculous feat.

Then, with a mighty roar, Hanuman leapt into the air. The vanaras watching from the shore cheered as he soared above them, his body like a streak of lightning, cutting through the sky. His leap was so powerful that it seemed to split the heavens and earth themselves. The ocean beneath him roiled with the force of his departure, as though nature itself was in awe of the mighty vanara's strength.

As Hanuman soared through the air, he passed clouds and mountains, his figure becoming a blur in the distance. The ocean, vast and deep, stretched before him, but Hanuman was undeterred. His leap seemed to carry him across the world itself, transcending boundaries, as he surged onward with single-minded determination.

The Ocean's Challenge

As Hanuman neared the midpoint of the ocean, he encountered a formidable obstacle—Surasa, the mother of all serpents. A great demoness who lived in the ocean, Surasa saw Hanuman as a challenge to her power. With a voice that echoed like thunder, she rose from the depths of the ocean, blocking his path.

"Who dares to cross my waters?" Surasa's voice boomed, filling the air with an unsettling chill. "I am Surasa, the guardian of the seas. Only those who can defeat me may pass."

Hanuman, ever fearless and composed, met Surasa's gaze. "I seek only to fulfill a mission entrusted to me by Rama. I ask for nothing more than to pass through your waters."

Surasa, however, was not easily swayed. "To pass me, you must first show your strength. Only then may you proceed."

Without hesitation, Hanuman's body began to expand, growing to an enormous size that dwarfed even Surasa. His strength radiated outward, as though the earth itself bent to his will. Surasa, undeterred, also began to expand, stretching her mouth wide to swallow the mighty vanara whole.

In an instant, Hanuman contracted his body to a tiny form, slipping effortlessly through Surasa's wide-open mouth, and then expanding once more to his normal size. Surasa, unable to catch him, saw the futility of her efforts. She nodded in approval and allowed him to pass.

"Go forth, O mighty Hanuman," she said, "for your strength is unparalleled. May you succeed in your mission."

With that, Hanuman continued his journey, soaring through the skies above the ocean, leaving the daunting challenge behind him.

Infiltrating Ravana's Court

As Hanuman neared the shores of Lanka, he could see the magnificent city of Ravana—towering, majestic, and brimming with opulence. The golden spires of Ravana's palace glimmered in the sunlight, reflecting the might and grandeur of the demon king. But Hanuman's mission was not one of conquest—it was one of intelligence and stealth.

He landed just outside the gates of Lanka, where the air was thick with the scent of flowers and incense. Though the city was beautiful, Hanuman's focus was unwavering. He needed to find Sita and bring back news of her location to Rama. Disguising himself as a tiny monkey, Hanuman crept through the shadows, using his speed and agility to move unnoticed.

As he ventured deeper into the city, Hanuman marveled at the sights around him. The courtyards were lush with vibrant flowers, and the roads were lined with statues of deities and kings. The air seemed thick with the riches of Ravana's reign, but Hanuman's mind remained fixed on his purpose.

It wasn't long before Hanuman reached the inner chambers of Ravana's palace, where he found Sita. There, sitting in a garden filled with fragrant flowers, was the beloved princess of Mithila. Her beauty, though diminished by sorrow, still radiated in the way the moon shines through a cloudy sky. She was surrounded by Ravana's guards, who were keeping a watchful eye on her.

Sita, as if sensing Hanuman's presence, looked up. She was filled with a mixture of surprise and hope. Her eyes, though weary from the trials she had endured, brightened for a moment when she saw Hanuman. He was the first person from her home, her beloved Rama, to appear before her in months.

"Who are you, O gentle creature?" Sita asked, her voice soft yet filled with curiosity.

Hanuman bowed before her respectfully, his heart full of compassion. "I am Hanuman, servant of Rama, and I come with news of your husband. He has not forgotten you, and he is coming to rescue you from Ravana's grasp."

Sita's face lit up with a mixture of joy and disbelief. "Rama is coming?" she whispered, her heart swelling with hope. "My Lord is near?"

Hanuman nodded solemnly. "He is, Sita. He will not rest until you are safe."

The Message for Rama

Before Hanuman left, he gave Sita a token—a ring from Rama, a symbol of his eternal love and devotion. "Take this to remind you that Rama has not forgotten you," he said, his voice filled with tenderness.

With that, Hanuman took his leave, his heart buoyed by the knowledge that he had successfully located Sita. But there was still much to be done. The journey was far from over, and the battle that lay ahead was one that would require all of their strength and courage.

Hanuman leapt once more into the sky, his heart filled with the promise of the triumph to come. The search for Sita had brought him to Lanka, and now he would return to Rama with the most crucial news of all—the location of his beloved wife.

Dadaji smiled at Parth as he closed the story. "This, my boy, is the turning point of the story. Hanuman's leap across the ocean was not just an incredible feat of strength—it was the moment when hope was reignited. It showed Rama that his mission was not just a dream. The forces of nature, and even the gods, were on his side."

Parth listened intently, his eyes wide with excitement. "What happened after Hanuman returned, Dadaji? How did Rama react?"

Dadaji chuckled softly. "Ah, Parth, the battle for Lanka was about to begin. And with Hanuman's arrival back in the camp, Rama and his allies were ready to face Ravana's might..."

And with that, the journey of Rama, Lakshmana, and Hanuman continued—a journey that would lead them to a showdown with the greatest demon king the world had ever known.

CHAPTER TWELVE

THE WRATH OF THE VANARA: LANKA ABLAZE

Hanuman's Defiance in Ravana's Court

As Hanuman made his way back to Lanka after meeting Sita, the journey had been full of purpose and triumph. He had completed the task that Rama had set before him—finding Sita, reassuring her of Rama's love, and delivering the ring that would serve as a token of his undying devotion. But Hanuman's mission was far from over. The moment of reckoning was still to come, for Ravana, the demon king, would not release Sita willingly. Before he could return to Rama with the news of his success, Hanuman had one more challenge to face: Ravana's court.

Hanuman, as mighty as he was, knew that the time had come for a show of strength and defiance. The vanara prince was a being of great power, and as the emissary of Rama, he had to send Ravana a message that no force could stand in the way of the divine plan that was unfolding. His loyalty to Rama was unwavering, and he would not let Ravana's arrogance go unchallenged.

Ravana's palace was a marvel of grandeur, built with the finest materials from across the three worlds. Its towering walls were adorned with jewels that gleamed like stars in the night sky. The king of Lanka, seated upon a throne that seemed to emanate an aura of dark power, ruled with an iron fist. His court, filled with rakshasas, warriors, and ministers, stood in silent awe of the mighty king.

But when Hanuman entered the court, his presence was like a storm. He was no longer the tiny creature who had slipped past the demonesses in Lanka. He had transformed, his form growing to a colossal size. As he entered the palace gates, the ground trembled beneath his feet. The rakshasas, who had previously laughed at his small stature, were now struck silent, their eyes wide in disbelief. Hanuman's every step seemed to shake the very foundations of Ravana's kingdom.

Ravana, enraged by Hanuman's boldness, rose from his throne. "Who dares to enter my court uninvited?" he thundered, his voice filled with venom.

Hanuman, standing tall and unyielding, met Ravana's gaze. His voice rang clear as he responded, "I am Hanuman, servant of Rama, and I have come to deliver a message. You have kidnapped Sita, and you will not escape the wrath of Rama. Release her now, or suffer the consequences."

Ravana's eyes flared with anger, and his voice, full of pride and contempt, echoed throughout the hall. "How dare you speak to me in such a manner, little monkey! You think you can challenge me, the king of Lanka? I will show you the true power of my kingdom."

The rakshasas around the court began to chant in support of their king, but Hanuman was undeterred. With a swift motion, he tore apart the magnificent golden gates of the palace, throwing them aside like mere twigs. His roar of defiance echoed throughout the kingdom, shaking Lanka to its core.

"You think you can stop Rama's will?" Hanuman said, his voice filled with righteous fury. "I will leave my mark on this city, a reminder of the power of dharma. You cannot hide from what is destined."

The rakshasas, realizing that Hanuman was not one to be trifled with, began to approach him with weapons raised. But before they could strike, Hanuman leapt into the air, his body growing larger with each passing second. In his mighty form, he swiped his tail across the city, toppling the finest structures of Lanka. The buildings shook and crumbled, and the once-mighty city of Ravana began to fall apart before Hanuman's wrath.

In a moment of sheer defiance, Hanuman plucked a burning branch from one of the fallen structures and set fire to the city. The flames spread quickly, licking the heavens as the buildings burned to the ground. Ravana, watching his city be reduced to ashes, was consumed with rage. His court had turned into chaos, as rakshasas rushed to extinguish the flames that were consuming their precious city.

Hanuman, however, was not finished. As the fire spread, he leapt from building to building, striking down any rakshasa who dared approach him. His mighty roar filled the air as he continued to destroy the heart of Ravana's kingdom. The burning city was a testament to the power of Rama and the wrath of dharma. Hanuman had sent a clear message: Ravana's time was running out.

The Return to Rama

Once his task was complete, Hanuman, his mission now accomplished, began his journey back to Rama. The burning city of Lanka was behind him, but the weight of his actions remained. As he crossed the vast ocean once more, the image of the ravaged city lingered in his mind. It was not just a physical destruction; it was the beginning of the end for Ravana. The flames had set fire to the very soul of the demon king's arrogance, and now, the path was clear for Rama's triumph.

Hanuman's heart swelled with anticipation as he neared the shores where Rama awaited him. He had accomplished what seemed impossible. He had found Sita, delivered the message of

Rama's love, and shown Ravana the might of the divine plan that would soon come to fruition.

As Hanuman touched the ground, his form returning to its original size, he was greeted with jubilation by Rama and his army of vanaras. The air was filled with cheers, as the brothers, Sugriva, and the entire army celebrated Hanuman's safe return.

Rama's eyes shone with pride as he looked at Hanuman. "My faithful servant," he said, his voice filled with deep emotion, "you have brought back more than just news of Sita's whereabouts. You have shown the strength and courage that will carry us to victory. The fire that now burns in Lanka is but a reflection of the fire in our hearts. The time for Ravana's defeat is upon us."

Hanuman, bowing before Rama, replied with humility, "Rama, your mission is my mission. Your victory is my victory. I am but a humble servant of your divine will. I shall never rest until Sita is returned to you."

With Hanuman's return, Rama's hope was reignited. The flames that had consumed Lanka were not just a symbol of destruction; they were a harbinger of the ultimate triumph of good over evil. Ravana's power, though great, was no match for the righteousness that Rama represented.

As the sun began to set on that fateful day, the vanara army gathered in anticipation of the battle to come. The burning of Lanka had sent a clear message, and the forces of evil would soon face the might of dharma.

Dadaji paused, looking at Parth with a gleam in his eyes. "And so, my boy, the stage was set for the final battle. Hanuman had struck the first blow. The burning of Lanka was a declaration—a declaration that the forces of righteousness would not rest until Ravana's tyranny was brought to an end."

Parth, his face alight with excitement, asked eagerly, "What happened next, Dadaji? How did the battle unfold?"

Dadaji smiled, his voice low and filled with anticipation. "Ah, Parth, that is a tale for the next chapter. The battle between Rama and Ravana was one for the ages. But it was not just a battle of strength; it was a battle of ideals, of dharma against adharma. And soon, the world would know the true power of Rama's resolve."

With that, the story continued—one that would change the course of history and shape the destiny of the world forever.

CHAPTER THIRTEEN

BRIDGING THE DIVIDE: THE PATH TO LANKA

The Construction of the Bridge to Lanka with the Help of the Vanaras

After the fiery events in Ravana's court, the time had come for Rama's army to take the next crucial step in their mission to rescue Sita: crossing the vast ocean that lay between them and the island kingdom of Lanka. However, the ocean, with its unyielding waves and endless stretch, posed a challenge that could not be easily overcome. But where there was a will, there was a way, and the vanaras, with their boundless energy and determination, were ready to take on the impossible task.

As Rama stood on the shores of the southern tip of India, his gaze fixed on the distant shores of Lanka, he knew that the moment had come. His army was strong, but the vast expanse of the ocean separated them from the battle that would decide the fate of Sita and the future of the world. The task was monumental, but not impossible. Rama's thoughts turned to the strength and resourcefulness of his vanara army. Together, they would build a bridge to cross the ocean and bring the fight to Ravana.

The great monkey king, Sugriva, stood by Rama's side, his eyes filled with unwavering loyalty and determination. "Rama," Sugriva said, "we will construct the bridge. The vanaras are ready to work together to make the impossible possible. We will find a way to reach Lanka and bring Sita back."

Rama nodded, his heart filled with gratitude. "I have faith in you, Sugriva, and in every vanara who stands with us. Together, we will show the world that no obstacle is too great when righteousness is at stake."

The plan was set into motion. The vanaras, under the guidance of Rama and Sugriva, began to gather the materials they would need for the bridge. Huge boulders, rocks, trees, and logs were collected from the nearby forests. The strength of the vanaras was legendary, and as they worked together, the task seemed less daunting with every passing moment. Rocks were tossed into the sea, trees were felled and floated across the waves, and massive logs were tied together with ropes made from vines.

The scene was one of awe and wonder. The vanaras worked tirelessly, their speed and strength seemingly boundless. It was as if the entire forest had come to life, with the vanaras moving as one cohesive force. Every effort was made with precision, as they knew that the success of this task would determine the outcome of the war. With every stone placed, every tree felled, and every log tied, the bridge grew stronger, inch by inch, stretching across the ocean.

Among the vanaras, a great sense of camaraderie flourished. Each member, from the mightiest warriors to the smallest of monkeys, played their part. Even Hanuman, whose strength was unmatched, worked alongside the others. His leaps through the air, carrying massive boulders, were a sight to behold. The sight of his gigantic form carrying stones as if they were mere pebbles inspired the vanaras to work even harder.

As the bridge took shape, it seemed as though the forces of nature themselves were supporting the vanaras. The waves of the ocean, which had once seemed so impassable, now seemed to part in reverence. The wind carried the scent of victory, and the sun shone brightly over the construction, as if blessing the efforts of the vanaras.

One by one, the vanaras placed their stones and boulders into the water, and the bridge began to rise from the ocean floor. It was no longer just a dream; it was becoming a reality. The bridge, made of earth and stone, had begun to take shape, stretching across the waters, connecting the land of India to the distant shores of Lanka.

Rama, watching from the shore, felt a surge of pride and gratitude. The vanaras were not just his allies; they were his brothers in arms, each one willing to give their all for the cause of righteousness. Together, they had overcome impossible odds, and now, with the bridge nearly complete, the final act of the mission was within reach.

The Thrilling March of Rama's Army Across the Ocean

As the final stones were placed, and the bridge to Lanka stood completed, a profound silence fell over the vanara army. The ocean, once an impassable barrier, now lay open before them, and the moment had come for the army to march forward.

Rama, his face radiant with hope and resolve, turned to his army. "The bridge is built, my friends. Now, we march. Let us show Ravanathe might of dharma and the power of unity. The time to rescue Sita has come."

With these words, Rama led the charge, and the vanaras followed, their spirits high, their hearts filled with purpose. The sight of the vast army marching across the bridge was a momentous one. It was as if the very earth had opened up to allow the forces of good to march forward, unstoppable and united in purpose.

The bridge stretched before them, its path illuminated by the light of the sun and the determination in the hearts of the soldiers. As Rama, Lakshmana, Sugriva, and Hanuman led the charge, their army followed, with thousands of vanaras, bears, and monkeys marching alongside them. The roar of their voices echoed across the sea, signaling the strength of their resolve.

Rama, his bow resting on his shoulder, walked with a steady and confident pace. His eyes were fixed on the distant shore of Lanka, where Sita was held captive. His heart burned with the desire to rescue her, to bring her back to the world of righteousness and truth. As he walked, the wind seemed to whisper his name, carrying the sound of his promise to his beloved Sita: "I will come for you. I will not rest until you are safe."

The vanaras, too, marched with pride. They knew that the task before them was not just one of physical strength but of spiritual resolve. The forces of evil, represented by Ravana and his army, would be met with the full force of dharma. The vanaras had built this bridge not just with their hands, but with their hearts, and their loyalty to Rama and the cause of righteousness was unwavering.

As they crossed the bridge, the sea beneath them seemed to reflect the unity and strength of the army. The water, once an obstacle, now seemed to support their every step, as if the very forces of nature were on their side. The journey across the ocean was filled with anticipation and determination, for each step brought them closer to Lanka, to the final battle, and to the rescue of Sita.

Rama, his heart heavy with love and hope, glanced over his shoulder at his army. "We march forward, for the victory of dharma," he said, his voice ringing with authority and conviction.

The vanaras, with their energy renewed, redoubled their efforts. Together, they moved forward with the force of a great wave, unstoppable and fierce. The battle ahead would be their ultimate test, but they knew that as long as they stood together, they would be victorious.

With each passing moment, the shores of Lanka drew nearer, and the vanara army pressed on, their resolve unbroken. The sound of their march was like the roar of the ocean itself, and the sky above seemed to tremble with the promise of the battle to come. The bridge was not just a physical structure—it was a symbol of hope, of unity, and of the triumph of good over evil.

As they neared the shores of Lanka, the army could already see the towering spires of Ravana's palace in the distance. The final confrontation was close at hand. And with every step they took, they were closer to fulfilling Rama's vow—to bring Sita back and to defeat the forces of darkness that threatened the world.

Parth, eyes wide with excitement, turned to his grandfather. "Dadaji, what happened next? What was the battle like?"

Dadaji smiled, his voice filled with pride. "Ah, Parth, that is a story for the next chapter. The battle that would unfold on the shores of Lanka would shake the heavens themselves. But the bridge we crossed—built with courage and unity—was the first victory in a war that would determine the fate of the world. But there is more to come, and the tale is far from over."

And so, the story of Rama, his army, and their journey to Lanka continued—each step bringing them closer to the final battle, the moment when destiny would unfold.

WAR OF LEGENDS: THE BATTLE BEGINS

It was the dawn of a day filled with uncertainty and anticipation. Dadaji sat back on his creaky old chair, the sounds of the morning breeze rustling the leaves of the banyan tree overhead. His eyes sparkled as he began to speak, his voice steady, yet brimming with the tension of the story he was about to tell.

"Parth," Dadaji began, as the young boy sat attentively at his feet, "you've heard about the great battle that took place in Lanka, haven't you? The one between Lord Rama and Ravana, the demon king. But do you know, my child, that the real war had already begun before the first arrow was ever released? It started with a thousand small skirmishes, each one a story in itself."

Parth nodded, the wind from the tree lifting his hair, his eyes wide with curiosity.

"You see," Dadaji continued, "Rama's army, though vast and mighty, was not the same as Ravana's. The forces of Ravana were known for their sheer strength and the dark magic they wielded. His army of rakshasas, demons with monstrous power, were not easily defeated. But Rama had something they did not—an army of unwavering loyalty and hearts full of dharma. It was the beginning of something far greater than just a battle—it was the clash of righteousness against evil."

The old man's gaze deepened, his voice turning softer as he delved into the story.

"It began with the first clash, Parth," he said. "The army of Rama, led by the valiant Lakshmana, surged forward to meet the oncoming rakshasa warriors. The first skirmish was like a storm—quick, fierce, and unrelenting."

Initial Skirmishes Between Rama's Forces and Ravana's Army

As Dadaji spoke, he painted a vivid picture of the battlefield, the colors of the dawn spreading across the horizon. In the distance, the army of Ravana stood like a wall of darkness, their eyes burning with malevolent fire. On the other side, the vanaras (monkey warriors) assembled with a fierce determination, their hearts unwavering despite the overwhelming odds.

Rama, standing tall with his bow in hand, was the epitome of calm amidst the chaos. His army, though outnumbered, was filled with warriors who fought not just for victory, but for the restoration of dharma.

"Lakshmana, with his fiery spirit, led the first charge. He was a whirlwind of action, his bow releasing arrows faster than a tempest," Dadaji said. "With every strike, the rakshasas faltered, but their numbers seemed endless."

Parth leaned forward. "But Dadaji, weren't they outnumbered? How did Rama's army even stand a chance?"

Dadaji smiled, his voice rich with wisdom. "Ah, my child, remember this—the size of an army is not what makes it powerful. It's the courage, the will to fight for what is right. And Rama's forces had that. The vanaras, led by Sugriva and Hanuman, fought with unparalleled bravery, while the divine archers like Angada stood as an unbreakable shield."

He paused, allowing the weight of his words to settle. "In those first skirmishes, Parth, it was not just strength that won the day—it was their unshakable belief in their cause."

Heroic Moments from Characters Like Angada and Sugriva

As Dadaji spoke, the scene of the battle unfolded in Parth's mind like a grand tapestry. The war was not just a battle between two armies; it was a clash of ideologies, a struggle for justice.

"Among the warriors who shone brightly in those early moments," Dadaji continued, "was Angada, the son of Vali. Angada was fearless, his heart burning with a desire to avenge his father's death. When the rakshasas came charging toward him, he stood his ground. One by one, he felled them with arrows that seemed to carry the very weight of his grief and anger."

Parth gasped. "Angada was that powerful?"

Dadaji nodded. "Yes, my child. Angada's power wasn't just physical. It was the strength of his conviction that made him a force to be reckoned with. He fought not only for himself but for the memory of his father. And in every arrow he shot, the weight of justice was carried."

He paused, letting the image of Angada's bravery sink into Parth's mind. "Then there was Sugriva. The vanara king, who had once been a prince in his own right, driven into exile by his own brother. Sugriva was no ordinary warrior. His strength was as legendary as his intelligence."

Dadaji's voice softened, his eyes distant as if remembering the moment vividly. "Sugriva, with his massive arms, fought side by side with the vanaras, his every move calculated. He knew how to strike at the right moment, never giving the rakshasas a chance to regroup. His bravery was in his strategy, not just in his strength."

Turning the Tide

Parth was completely engrossed in the tale now. He could almost hear the clash of weapons, the cries of warriors, and the thundering roars of the rakshasas as they tried to break through Rama's lines.

"And then, just when the tide of battle seemed to turn in favor of Ravana's forces, something changed. The warriors of Lanka were fierce, but their hearts were cold. And that," Dadaji said, leaning forward slightly, "is where the real power of Rama's army lay—in their hearts."

He continued, his voice rising with passion, "Rama's warriors, the vanaras, the bears, and the great allies of the gods, fought not just for glory, but for the righteousness of their cause. Every swing of their mace, every arrow from their bow, carried with it the strength of dharma itself."

Dadaji smiled at Parth's awe-stricken face. "You see, Parth, the strength of a warrior is not always in his weapon or his size. Sometimes, it lies in the purity of his heart and the strength of his belief."

The battle raged on, but Dadaji could sense the young boy's spirit soaring with the heroes of the Ramayana.

"Now," Dadaji said, his tone softening, "the true test for Rama's army was just beginning. The road ahead was long, and the trials many. But with warriors like Angada, Sugriva, and Hanuman by his side, Rama knew that victory was within reach—not just for him, but for the entire world."

Dadaji leaned back in his chair, his eyes twinkling with the depth of the story's unfolding. "So you see, Parth, the first steps in the battle for Lanka were more than just a series of skirmishes. They were the beginning of the triumph of good over evil. They were the first whispers of victory."

Parth sat in deep thought, his young mind grasping the importance of what he had just heard. "So, the real strength, Dadaji, is in believing in what's right?"

"Exactly, my boy," Dadaji said softly. "The right path is always the hardest to walk, but it is the one that leads to true victory."

The sun was beginning to set, casting long shadows beneath the old banyan tree. As the evening breeze swept through the leaves, Parth felt a sense of peace settle over him. He now understood what it meant to be truly brave, truly heroic.

And so, with each new battle, Rama's army inched closer to their goal, and with each new victory, they proved that righteousness could never be defeated, no matter how fierce the darkness that stood against it.

CHAPTER FIFTEEN

THE FINAL HOUR: RAVANA'S DEFEAT

The air was thick with tension, the ground trembling as two mighty forces stood on the battlefield. Rama's army, resolute and unyielding, faced the overwhelming power of Ravana'srakshasa forces. Dadaji leaned forward, his eyes reflecting the weight of the moment, his voice carrying the weight of history.

"Parth," Dadaji began, his tone filled with solemnity, "what you are about to hear is not just the story of a battle. It is the story of a divine clash between good and evil, where the very fate of the world hung in the balance."

Parth, wide-eyed and entranced by the gravity of his grandfather's words, leaned in closer, eager to listen.

"Rama had already fought many battles. His army had crossed oceans, faced demons, and endured countless trials. But none of this had prepared him for the final confrontation with Ravana, the king of Lanka. This," Dadaji paused for effect, "was a battle that would decide the very fate of dharma itself."

The Climactic Battle Between Rama and Ravana

The battlefield, Parth, was a sight to behold. Imagine a vast expanse, stretching as far as the eye could see, filled with the clang of weapons and the cries of warriors. On one side stood Rama, tall and unwavering, his bow gleaming in the sunlight. His warriors, though tired from days of battle, were filled with unwavering resolve. And on the other side, Ravana, the mighty king of Lanka, stood surrounded by his fearsome rakshasas, each one more terrifying than the last.

"Ravana, Parth," Dadaji continued, "was a king like no other. His power was unmatched. His army, vast and monstrous, seemed invincible. He had ten heads, each one representing a different aspect of his mind—intellect, desire, and strength."

Parth, fascinated, asked, "How could anyone defeat such a powerful enemy, Dadaji?"

Dadaji smiled gently. "Ah, my child, power can be deceiving. Ravana's greatest strength was also his greatest weakness. His arrogance, his belief that he could never be defeated, clouded his judgment. He thought his strength made him invincible. But as we know, Parth, arrogance always leads to downfall."

The Beginning of the Final Duel

The moment of reckoning arrived as Rama and Ravana faced each other on the battlefield. The world seemed to stand still. The sun had barely risen, but the clouds above churned with the promise of an epic storm.

Rama, with his serene composure, raised his bow. The warriors around him, their hearts filled with courage, held their breath. Ravana, on the other hand, was consumed by fury. His ten heads twisted and turned, each one muttering a different chant, his hands ready to unleash his dark powers.

Dadaji's voice grew more intense as he described the start of the battle. "With a cry that shook the heavens, Ravana charged at Rama, his mighty sword held high. But Rama, with his unfaltering calm, drew his bow. The first arrow he released was like the roar of thunder, its aim true, but Ravana was quick to block it with his own shield."

The battle began in earnest, Parth, with each warrior bringing all their might to the fight. Rama's arrows struck like lightning, each one seeking the heart of the demon king's forces. But Ravana was not one to go down easily. His strength was immense, and his magic potent.

"Ravana's strength, Parth, lay in his mastery of the dark arts. He could summon storms, control fire, and had the power to turn invisible. But Rama was not daunted. His arrows, blessed by the gods, were guided by dharma itself."

Dadaji paused, allowing the story to unfold in the boy's mind. "You see, Parth, Ravana's strength was physical and magical, but Rama's strength was spiritual. And that made all the difference."

Battle Strategies: The Clash of Titans

The battle raged on, and Dadaji described the intricate strategies of both sides. "Rama, though powerful, knew that defeating Ravana was not a simple task. He had to be smart, patient. Every time Ravana unleashed his magic, Rama would counter with precision."

As the two titans clashed, Dadaji's voice turned more animated, illustrating the stunning imagery of the battle. "Rama's army was not just a force of might. It was a force of intelligence and unity. While Ravana relied on his strength, Rama relied on his strategy. His warriors—Hanuman, Sugriva, Angada—fought with the precision of a well-oiled machine."

"The battle strategies were astounding, Parth. Hanuman and the vanaras took on Ravana'srakshasas with their cunning and bravery. Angada, driven by his father's memory, fought valiantly, striking down the demons one by one. Sugriva, the vanara king, displayed unmatched agility, charging through the enemy lines."

Dadaji's tone shifted as he described Rama's next move. "But Rama knew the key to victory lay in Ravana's vulnerability—the ten heads. Each head, while powerful, had its own weaknesses. Ravana had hidden his most vulnerable spot deep within his heart. And Rama, with his divine insight, knew just where to strike."

Ravana's Ultimate Downfall

The battle had reached its peak. Both armies were exhausted, their strength waning, but the fight for victory was far from over. Dadaji's voice became even more dramatic as he recounted the decisive moment.

"Rama, in the midst of the battle, saw his chance. With a prayer to Lord Vishnu, he drew his most powerful arrow—a weapon blessed by the gods themselves. He aimed with precision, his eyes focused solely on Ravana's heart. The moment the arrow left his bow, time seemed to stop. It sailed through the air with the speed of lightning, striking Ravana's chest."

Parth gasped, caught up in the moment. "Did it kill Ravana, Dadaji?"

"Yes," Dadaji said softly, "It pierced Ravana's heart, the final blow to the mighty king. Ravana's ten heads fell to the ground, one by one, and with them, the last vestiges of his arrogance."

The Aftermath

As Ravana fell, the ground shook, and the sky darkened for a moment. But soon, the clouds parted, and the sun broke through, as though the heavens themselves were rejoicing in Ravana's defeat. Dadaji's voice became gentler as he spoke of the aftermath.

"The battle was over, but the war was won, not just by Rama's might, but by the triumph of dharma over adharma. Ravana's reign had been a dark one, but with his defeat, light returned to the world."

Parth sat still, his young mind grappling with the weight of the story. "So, Rama won because he was fighting for what was right?"

Dadaji nodded. "Exactly, my child. In the end, it is not strength alone that determines victory. It is the righteousness of the cause that ensures true triumph."

As Dadaji finished, the wind had died down, and the evening was settling into a peaceful silence. Parth sat for a moment, lost in thought, before looking up at his grandfather.

"Rama's victory wasn't just over Ravana, was it, Dadaji?" he asked.

"No, Parth," Dadaji replied with a knowing smile. "It was a victory over every force that seeks to destroy dharma. And that is why we remember it, even today."

CHAPTER SIXTEEN

THROUGH THE FIRE: SITA'S TRIAL OF PURITY

The sun had dipped below the horizon, casting long shadows across the land. The air was still, as though the world itself held its breath, waiting for the events to unfold. Dadaji sat in his chair, his eyes gazing into the distance as though he could see the very landscape of Lanka before him. His voice was soft but firm, carrying with it the gravity of the story.

"Parth," he began, his tone laden with both sorrow and hope, "what you are about to hear is not just about a trial of fire. It is about the strength of the soul, the purity of the heart, and the ultimate test of faith."

Parth, who had been listening intently, now leaned forward, sensing that the story was about to take a dramatic turn. "What happened, Dadaji?" he asked, eager to understand.

Dadaji's eyes softened, and he began, "Sita, the daughter of the earth, had endured much during her time in Ravana's captivity. When Rama defeated Ravana and liberated her, there was an unspoken question lingering in the air. Could a woman, held captive for so long by a demon king, remain pure in heart and spirit? Was she untouched by the darkness of her captor's palace?"

Parth felt the tension in the air, as though he too were standing on the precipice of the moment.

Sita's Ordeal by Fire

Dadaji's voice grew heavier as he continued, "Rama, despite his deep love for Sita, had his doubts. The people of Ayodhya, influenced by the whispers of the world, were not as forgiving. They questioned Sita's purity, her honor, after being in Ravana's palace for so long."

"Was it really necessary for her to prove her purity, Dadaji?" Parth interrupted, his voice filled with confusion.

Dadaji sighed, "It is difficult, my child. In those times, the honor of a woman was often questioned based on circumstances beyond her control. Despite the fact that Sita had never wavered in her devotion to Rama, the doubt in the hearts of the people grew. Rama, as a king, had to uphold the dignity of his throne and the faith of his kingdom."

"Rama had never doubted Sita's love or purity in his heart. He knew her to be the embodiment of virtue. But the voice of the people was loud, and as a ruler, he had to listen to their concerns. He could not afford to let doubt take root in the kingdom."

Dadaji paused, allowing the weight of the situation to settle in Parth's heart. "And so, with a heavy heart, Rama decided that Sita would undergo the Agni Pariksha—the trial by fire. If she was pure, the fire would have no power over her. If she was impure, the flames would consume her."

The Trial Before the Fire

The day arrived, Parth, when Sita was to face her trial. A grand pyre was prepared in the center of the kingdom, surrounded by thousands of onlookers. The air was thick with anticipation, and Sita, draped in her royal garments, stood silently before the flames.

"Imagine this moment, Parth," Dadaji said, his voice trembling with the weight of what had transpired. "Here stood Sita, not as a prisoner of Ravana, but as a queen, the beloved wife of Rama, and yet, she was about to face the harshest test of all—one that no woman should ever have to endure."

Parth could feel the intensity of the moment, the sorrow of it, even though it was a story of the past. "What did she feel, Dadaji?" he asked softly.

Dadaji's eyes softened with understanding. "Sita, my child, was a woman of unmatched strength. She had endured countless trials. Her heart remained pure, untouched by the darkness of Ravana's captivity. She knew that she had never faltered in her devotion to Rama. But the flames of the Agni Pariksha were not just a test of her physical purity. They were a test of her spirit, her trust in her dharma."

As the pyre was lit, the flames leaped high into the sky, casting a golden glow across the land. Sita stepped forward, her heart calm, her eyes unwavering. She was not afraid. With every step, she seemed to draw closer to her destiny, the very purpose of her existence.

"Rama, my love, I trust in the fire," Sita whispered to herself, her voice a prayer, a plea, a declaration of faith.

The Divine Proof of Purity

Dadaji's voice became filled with awe as he continued, "As the flames rose higher, everyone watched in suspense. The fire danced around her, threatening to consume her very being. But when Sita stepped into the flames, something miraculous happened."

"Was she hurt?" Parth asked, his voice filled with concern.

"No," Dadaji replied, his eyes twinkling. "The fire did not touch her. The flames parted before her, as though they recognized her purity, her devotion, her strength. And from the heart of the fire, the Earth herself, the very mother who had birthed Sita, rose up. She called upon Sita and said, 'You are pure, my child. No harm shall come to you. You have proven your virtue.'"

A stunned silence fell over the crowd as the divine voice of the Earth echoed through the air. The fire, which had been threatening to consume Sita, now seemed like a symbol of her purity. Her ordeal had ended, not in defeat, but in triumph.

The Emotional Reunion of Rama and Sita

As the flames died down and the smoke cleared, the crowd stood in awe. Sita emerged from the fire, her form radiant, untouched by the flames, as though she had been blessed by the gods themselves. Her face was serene, her eyes filled with grace and wisdom, yet there was an undeniable sadness in them, for she knew the depth of the trial she had just endured.

Dadaji's voice softened as he spoke of the reunion. "Rama stood there, watching the woman he loved emerge from the fire, knowing that she was pure. Yet, the question of his own heart lingered. He too had faced the pressure of the people, the burden of leadership. And so, with a heart full of love, but weighed down by duty, he turned to Sita."

"'Sita,' he said, his voice filled with sorrow and admiration, 'you have passed the test. You have proven your purity, your strength. But the world will not understand. I must now ask you to return to the Earth, where you came from, for the sake of the kingdom.'"

Parth gasped, unable to comprehend what he was hearing. "What do you mean, Dadaji? Why did Rama ask her to leave?"

Dadaji's eyes grew heavy with sadness as he explained, "Because, Parth, even though Sita had proven her purity, the world's doubts would never be silenced. The pain of it tore at Rama's heart, but as a king, he had to make the ultimate sacrifice for the greater good. He believed that for the peace of the kingdom, Sita would have to return to the Earth, where she belonged."

Sita's Return to the Earth

Dadaji's voice dropped to a whisper as he concluded, "And so, Sita, with the same grace and dignity she had carried throughout her life, stepped into the Earth once more. Her mother, the Earth, called her home, and with that, Sita returned to her divine origin."

Parth sat in stunned silence, processing the magnitude of what his grandfather had just shared. "But didn't Rama love her, Dadaji?" he asked quietly.

Dadaji nodded slowly. "Rama's love for Sita was beyond measure. But the weight of duty, the pressure of his position as king, led him to make choices that even he could not escape. Yet, even as Sita returned to the Earth, it was clear that their love, their bond, could never be broken."

CHAPTER SEVENTEEN

THE RETURN OF THE KING: RAMA'S CORONATION

Dadaji settled into his chair, his voice lowering, almost as if he were recounting a sacred event, one that was both joyful and solemn. Parth, who had grown so used to the rhythm of his grandfather's storytelling, could tell that this chapter of the Ramayana was one of great significance. There was a calm in Dadaji'sdemeanor, as though he were about to tell a tale that held the promise of both triumph and wisdom.

"Parth," Dadaji began, "this chapter of the story is the culmination of everything Rama has gone through—his exile, his trials, his sacrifices. It is the moment when his patience, his devotion, and his adherence to dharma finally meet their reward. It is the return of the hero, the return of justice."

Parth listened intently, his eyes fixed on Dadaji. "What happened, Dadaji? Tell me more."

Rama's Triumphant Return to Ayodhya

The day that Rama, Sita, and Lakshmana returned to Ayodhya was unlike any other. After fourteen long years in the forest, battling demons and facing insurmountable odds, they were finally returning home. Rama had won a victory not only over Ravana, but over every challenge life had thrown his way.

"Can you imagine, Parth, what it must have been like for the people of Ayodhya?" Dadaji asked, his voice filled with a touch of awe. "The entire kingdom must have felt as if they had been waiting for ages for this moment. The streets of Ayodhya were lined with people, and the city itself seemed to glow with the light of hope and joy. It was as though the sun itself had returned to the earth."

Parth could almost feel the excitement and anticipation in the air, just as Dadaji described. "The people had longed for this day," Dadaji continued. "They had missed their prince, their rightful king. Now, they could finally see him again. The victory over Ravana was not just Rama's—it was theirs too. They had all suffered through the years of exile, the grief of losing their prince, and now it was time for their long-awaited reunion."

As the procession entered the city, it was clear that this was no ordinary homecoming. The air was filled with the sounds of drums and trumpets, the scent of flowers and incense, and the cheers of the people. Rama, the exiled prince, was finally home to claim his throne.

"Rama," Dadaji continued, "rode in a chariot, surrounded by his brothers, his wife, and his allies. The people of Ayodhya cheered, waving banners and throwing flowers. The streets were ablaze with the light of joy. It was not just a return; it was the return of righteousness, of dharma."

The Coronation Ceremony

But the story did not end with just the return. For this was the moment when Rama was to be crowned king of Ayodhya, to sit on the throne that was rightfully his. The people's joy had a purpose. They were not just celebrating his return; they were preparing for his coronation.

"Rama, my child, had always been a king in his heart," Dadaji said, his voice steady. "But the title of 'king' is not just a matter of having the right bloodline or winning a war. It is about being worthy of the crown. Rama had proven himself not only as a warrior but as a man of wisdom, compassion, and above all, dharma."

Parth nodded, understanding now the depth of the moment. The coronation was not just about a king sitting on a throne. It was a symbolic moment that marked the return of righteousness to the land. The people weren't just honoring a king; they were honoring dharma itself.

Rama stood before the people, his regal form illuminated by the setting sun. The golden chariot that had carried him into the city now stood in the palace courtyard, and the sacred ritual of the coronation was about to begin.

"The grand temple was filled with sages, priests, and the kingdom's elders," Dadaji continued. "Rama's father, King Dasharatha, though no longer alive, was honored in spirit. His blessing was invoked, for it was his desire that Rama take the throne. The entire city seemed to hold its breath as the ceremony began."

Rama stood tall, his face serene, but within him was the weight of years of struggle and sacrifice. Today was a moment of triumph, but it was also a moment of great responsibility. As he knelt before the sacred fire, the priests chanted mantras, offering prayers for his well-being and prosperity.

"In that moment, Parth, as Rama stood before the fire, he wasn't just a man. He was the embodiment of dharma, the promise of justice, and the hope of his people. And when the moment came, the sacred oil was poured over his head, and the people erupted in joyous cheers."

The Dawn of Rama Rajya

With the coronation complete, Rama was now king of Ayodhya, but what followed was more than just a formal declaration. It marked the beginning of a new era for the kingdom. It was the dawn of *Rama Rajya*—an era of peace, justice, and prosperity.

Dadaji's voice deepened with wisdom as he continued, "Rama Rajya was not just a kingdom. It was a vision—a vision of what a kingdom could be when ruled by dharma. Under Rama's rule, there was no oppression, no suffering, only fairness and righteousness. The land flourished. The people lived in peace. The courts were fair, the fields were fertile, and the hearts of the people were content."

Parth's mind swirled with the idea of such a kingdom. "Was Rama Rajya perfect, Dadaji?" he asked, eager to understand the true impact of Rama's reign.

Dadaji smiled gently. "Perfection, my child, is a faraway dream. But Rama Rajya came very close to it. It was a kingdom where the ruler's heart was aligned with the welfare of his people. It was a time when truth and justice prevailed over greed and deceit. The king was a servant to the people, and the people were the lifeblood of the kingdom. Rama's rule became a model, one that people would long remember for generations."

For a moment, Parth thought about the world around him—how different it was, yet how similar the desire for peace and justice remained. Dadaji's words seemed to echo in his heart. *Rama Rajya*—an era where dharma was supreme, where the rule of law was just and fair, where the people and the king walked hand in hand toward a shared vision of prosperity.

The Legacy of Rama's Rule

Dadaji's voice softened, as though he were speaking not just of Rama's reign, but of the lasting legacy it left behind. "Even now, Parth, people speak of *Rama Rajya* as the ideal. It is not just about a kingdom, but about the way we live our lives. It is about living with honor, with compassion, and with a sense of justice for all."

"The story of Rama's coronation, and the era that followed, teaches us that the highest good is not just about individual triumph, but about the well-being of everyone. Rama's reign was not about the glory of the king alone; it was about the flourishing of the people, the peace of the land, and the eternal truth of dharma."

Parth, though young, felt the weight of Dadaji's words. He understood, perhaps for the first time, that the ideals of the Ramayana were not just stories of gods and kings. They were lessons for life—lessons on how to live, how to rule, and how to be a good person in a world that often seemed full of challenges.

CHAPTER EIGHTEEN

THE ETERNAL LEGACY (EPILOGUE)

As the evening sun dipped behind the hills, casting long shadows across the garden, the air was heavy with a profound stillness. The soft rustling of the leaves in the wind seemed to echo the wisdom of ages past. Parth, still sitting cross-legged at the foot of the banyan tree, was deep in thought. His eyes flickered with the images of Rama, Sita, and the brave warriors who had taken part in the battle for dharma. The quiet hum of the evening enveloped him as Dadaji closed the ancient Ramayana book with a satisfied sigh.

Parth looked up at Dadaji, his mind swirling with questions, thoughts, and emotions that had formed throughout their conversations. "Dadaji," he began, his voice filled with a mix of awe and curiosity, "do you think the world can still follow the path of dharma, like Rama did?"

Dadaji's eyes twinkled with the wisdom of countless years. "Ah, Parth, that is the heart of the Ramayana itself, the eternal search for dharma—righteousness, duty, and truth. It is not just a story about gods and demons, but a reflection of the very human struggle between right and wrong. You see, dharma is not a destination, but a path. It's the journey of each person, each soul, to find their way through the challenges of life, just as Rama did."

He paused, leaning back against the tree, his fingers tracing the worn edges of the Ramayana's cover. "Rama faced incredible trials—exile, the loss of his wife, betrayal, and war. But through it all, he never swerved from his duty. His actions were a testament to what it means to be human. In a world where emotions can cloud our judgment, where anger, fear, and doubt often take the lead, dharma calls on us to rise above them."

Parth's gaze was fixed on Dadaji, but his mind was far away, deep within the tales of courage and sacrifice that had unfolded before him. "But what about the choices people make today, Dadaji? People still struggle with anger, fear, and doubts, don't they? In a world filled with distractions and challenges, where is the space for dharma?"

Dadaji smiled gently, understanding the depth of Parth's inquiry. He reached for his cup of tea, savoring its warmth before continuing. "Yes, Parth, the world has changed, but human nature, with all its flaws and virtues, remains the same. The struggle is still there. It might seem that in today's fast-paced, technology-driven world, the stories of old are far removed from our daily lives. But I tell you, every time you face a difficult decision, every time you act out of love, compassion, or duty, you are living dharma. Dharma is not bound by time—it is the essence that connects all beings, past and present."

Parth thought for a moment, his mind piecing together the wisdom Dadaji had shared. "So, even today, we can still make choices like Rama did? We can still follow the path of dharma?"

Dadaji nodded slowly, his voice calm but firm. "Indeed, you can. Every day, you are given the opportunity to make choices. The story of Rama is not meant to be a distant memory; it is a guide, a beacon that lights the way through the challenges of life. You may not face the same battles he did, but the essence of those trials—sacrifice, truth, and resilience—is still relevant. The dharma of a son, a friend, a ruler, or a warrior is ever-present."

Parth's thoughts drifted back to the many battles Rama had fought, both within himself and against external forces. His mind lingered on the way Rama had consistently chosen the right path, even when it was the hardest path to follow. He thought about

Sita's unwavering purity, about Lakshmana's unshakeable loyalty, and even Ravana's tragic fall—consumed by his own desires and ego. Parth began to understand that the Ramayana wasn't just a tale of gods; it was the story of every human soul, striving to find balance amidst chaos.

"But what about sacrifice, Dadaji?" Parth asked, almost hesitantly. "We've talked a lot about duty, but how can we learn to make sacrifices, like Rama did?"

Dadaji leaned forward slightly, his eyes reflecting the depth of his understanding. "Sacrifice is the essence of true strength, Parth. It is not about giving up something for the sake of loss, but for the greater good. Rama's exile, his separation from Sita, his battle with Ravana—all of these were sacrifices made for the benefit of dharma. They weren't easy. They were painful, and yet they were necessary."

He continued, his voice growing more reflective. "You see, the world often tells us that success is measured by what we gain—money, fame, power. But true success lies in what you are willing to give up, to protect something greater than yourself. That is the kind of sacrifice that leads to growth. Sacrifice is not about what you lose, but about what you gain in your heart, what you stand for, and the legacy you leave behind."

Parth sat quietly, processing Dadaji's words. He thought about his own life—the challenges he faced with school, with friendships, with family—and how often he found himself caught between doing what was easy and doing what was right. He wondered what it would take to have the courage to make sacrifices for a greater good, to choose dharma over immediate comfort or selfish desire.

Dadaji broke the silence, his tone soft yet filled with meaning. "Rama's story, Parth, is not just about him. It's about every soul that seeks to find the right path, despite the obstacles that arise. It is about resilience—the ability to stand strong in the face of adversity, to rise again when you fall, and to never lose sight of your values."

Parth's heart swelled with a newfound understanding. The values of dharma, sacrifice, and resilience weren't just ancient ideals—they were the very foundation of the human spirit. He felt a deep connection to the story of Rama, not just as a tale from the past, but as a living, breathing lesson that applied to his own life.

"Dadaji," Parth finally said, his voice full of wonder, "I want to learn more about these stories, about dharma, about the heroes of the past. I want to understand more, not just about Rama, but about the other figures, the lessons they taught, and how they can help me be better in the world today."

Dadaji smiled, his eyes glimmering with pride. "That, my dear Parth, is the true spirit of learning. The Ramayana is but one story, but it contains endless lessons that will guide you for a lifetime. And just as you've started to understand the lessons of dharma, sacrifice, and resilience, there are many more waiting for you in the ancient texts, in the wisdom of the sages, and in the stories of the great souls who walked this earth before us."

He leaned back against the tree, the golden hues of the setting sun now casting a warm glow on his face. "Never stop asking questions, Parth. Never stop seeking the truth. The stories of the past are not merely history; they are the keys to understanding the present and shaping the future. And the eternal legacy of dharma will always guide you."

Parth nodded thoughtfully, a sense of peace settling in his heart. The story of Rama had opened his eyes to a deeper understanding of life. He knew that the journey of learning had only just begun.

As the first stars began to twinkle in the night sky, Parth sat there, feeling a quiet excitement stir within him. The stories of the past were no longer just tales of adventure and heroism; they were now the guiding principles for his own life, a light to navigate the complexities of the world.

And so, as the wind whispered through the leaves, carrying with it the timeless lessons of the Ramayana, Parth's curiosity was ignited, and a new chapter of his own journey began.

CHAPTER NINETEEN

APPLYING ANCIENT WISDOM TO MODERN LIFE

The Ramayana, an epic woven with rich layers of philosophy, ethics, and virtues, offers timeless lessons that resonate deeply in today's world. While the story takes place in a mythical past, its characters embody ideals and qualities that continue to be relevant in our personal, professional, and societal lives. As we navigate the complexities of the modern world, the Ramayana's wisdom can help us address numerous challenges, from emotional intelligence and relationships to leadership, resilience, and ethical conduct.

1. Rama: The Ideal Leader and Upholder of Dharma

Lesson: Upholding duty (Dharma) and making ethical choices despite challenges.

Rama, the hero of the Ramayana, is often seen as the epitome of virtue, duty, and righteousness. As a prince, he was expected to uphold dharma (righteousness), and he did so with unwavering resolve, even when it meant personal suffering. His exile to the forest, his relentless pursuit to rescue Sita, and his battle with Ravana all demonstrate a deep commitment to his duties as a son, a brother, and a leader.

Application to Modern Life: In modern-day situations, we face complex ethical dilemmas that require us to choose between right and wrong, sometimes with no easy answers. Rama's unwavering commitment to dharma offers a powerful guide. In leadership roles, whether in business, government, or community organizations, we can take inspiration from Rama's ability to lead with integrity, prioritizing duty over personal gain. When making decisions, especially tough ones, it's crucial to ask: "What is the righteous thing to do, not just for me, but for the collective good?"

For instance, in the workplace, a leader may face pressure to compromise on values for the sake of profits or convenience. Following Rama's example, a leader who prioritizes ethics over expedience can build trust, inspire loyalty, and lead their teams with dignity. Rama's sacrifice of his personal comfort for the welfare of his kingdom teaches us that true leadership requires selflessness and the courage to stand by what is right, even at a personal cost.

2. Sita: The Embodiment of Strength, Purity, and Loyalty

Lesson: Strength in adversity and the importance of integrity and faithfulness.

Sita, the wife of Rama, stands as a symbol of purity, resilience, and loyalty. Her strength is not just physical, but emotional and spiritual. Throughout her trials, from being abducted by Ravana to undergoing the trial of fire (Agni Pariksha), Sita maintains her integrity and devotion. Her ability to endure suffering without losing her sense of self or her love for Rama teaches us profound lessons in resilience.

Application to Modern Life: In today's world, where stress, betrayal, and emotional challenges abound, Sita's character teaches us the power of inner strength and maintaining our integrity under pressure. In the face of adversity, especially in personal relationships, we often encounter situations where our values or faith are tested. Whether in a strained marriage, a friendship turned sour, or during times of public scrutiny, Sita's ability to uphold her purity and resilience in the face of severe challenges offers a powerful model.

Her journey highlights that resilience is not just about surviving difficulty but doing so while staying true to one's values. In a corporate context, individuals may face unethical situations, such as dishonesty or manipulation. Sita's unwavering commitment to her principles encourages us to remain steadfast and grounded, even when external forces try to sway us. Her devotion also underscores the importance of loyalty in relationships and the idea that true strength lies in emotional fortitude, not just in physical might.

3. Lakshmana: The Loyal Companion and Protector

Lesson: Loyalty, sacrifice, and the role of support in overcoming challenges.

Lakshmana, Rama's younger brother, epitomizes loyalty, sacrifice, and selflessness. His decision to accompany Rama into exile and his willingness to protect his brother and Sita at all costs speaks volumes about his character. Lakshmana's constant support, both physical and emotional, is a testament to the power of loyalty and dedication to those we care for.

Application to Modern Life: In modern relationships—whether familial, professional, or personal—the role of a supportive companion can make a significant difference. Lakshmana's character teaches us the value of being a loyal friend, partner, or colleague, especially when those we love or care about are going through challenging times. Whether supporting a spouse through a difficult career change or assisting a friend struggling with mental health, loyalty and sacrifice are essential qualities.

In professional settings, loyalty is often seen as an outdated concept, especially in a fast-paced world where career advancement sometimes encourages moving away from commitments. However,

Lakshmana's willingness to sacrifice personal comfort for the sake of his brother shows that sometimes the greatest rewards come from supporting others selflessly. This applies not only to familial relationships but to friendships and workplaces, where being a dependable and loyal individual fosters a sense of security and belonging.

4. Hanuman: Devotion, Courage, and the Power of Self-Belief

Lesson: The transformative power of devotion, courage, and self-belief.

Hanuman, the devoted monkey god, is perhaps one of the most beloved characters in the Ramayana. Known for his immense strength, wisdom, and unshakable devotion to Rama, Hanuman embodies the qualities of humility, courage, and selfless service. His most famous act, the leap to Lanka to deliver Rama's message to Sita, showcases not only his physical strength but also his belief in himself—something that was initially hidden by his own doubts.

Application to Modern Life: Hanuman's story teaches us about the importance of self-belief and perseverance, especially when faced with overwhelming odds. In today's competitive world, it's easy to feel insignificant or doubt our own abilities. Hanuman's realization of his own power after being reminded by Jambavan (the wise bear) that he could move mountains is a powerful metaphor for unlocking one's true potential.

In professional or personal endeavors, when we feel incapable of achieving something, Hanuman's example reminds us to trust in ourselves and to seek the courage to overcome obstacles. His devotion to Rama also emphasizes the importance of passion and purpose in our work and actions. Whether we are chasing a personal goal, embarking on a career, or tackling a creative project, Hanuman teaches us that devotion to a cause and unwavering belief in our abilities can lead to extraordinary achievements.

5. *Ravana: The Consequences of Ego and Desire*

Lesson: The destructive nature of unchecked ego and desire.

Ravana, the demon king of Lanka, is one of the most complex characters in the Ramayana. While a scholar, a ruler, and a powerful figure, Ravana's downfall comes as a result of his unchecked ego and insatiable desires, particularly his obsession with Sita. His actions, driven by pride and an inflated sense of self-importance, eventually lead to his destruction.

Application to Modern Life: In today's world, Ravana's story serves as a cautionary tale about the dangers of ego, greed, and unbridled desire. Whether in personal relationships or the corporate world, unchecked ambition and desire can lead to harmful consequences. Ravana's arrogance, his refusal to listen to wise counsel, and his inability to control his desires resulted in his undoing.

In business, for instance, leaders who place personal success above the welfare of others may face the collapse of their organization or relationships. In personal life, egos can ruin marriages, friendships, and familial bonds. Ravana's story reminds us of the importance of humility and the need to balance ambition with compassion and wisdom. The key takeaway here is that true greatness comes from understanding and managing one's desires and not allowing them to define our actions or decisions.

Conclusion: The Ramayana's Wisdom For Today's World

The characters of the Ramayana offer profound lessons that transcend time and space, providing insights into human nature, ethics, and resilience. Whether it's Rama's dedication to dharma, Sita's purity, Lakshmana's loyalty, Hanuman's devotion, or Ravana's tragic downfall due to ego, each character imparts valuable teachings that can be applied to solve modern-day problems. By embracing the principles of dharma, sacrifice, resilience, loyalty, and self-belief, we can navigate the complexities of contemporary life with grace, strength, and purpose.

In a world where the pace of life is often overwhelming and where challenges seem insurmountable, the stories of the Ramayana remind us of our capacity for greatness, provided we remain rooted in righteousness, humility, and wisdom.

Author's Note

Dear Reader,

It is with immense joy and a deep sense of purpose that I present this labor of love, *Ramayana Reimagined: The Eternal Legacy.* This book is not merely a retelling of an ancient epic but a journey—one that bridges the timeless wisdom of our heritage with the complexities of the modern world.

As a storyteller, I've always believed in the transformative power of narratives. The *Ramayana* is more than just a tale of heroism and devotion; it is a guide to navigating life's trials with grace, courage, and a steadfast commitment to dharma. Through its characters, each embodying virtues and flaws, the epic offers lessons that resonate across time and cultures.

In crafting this book, I chose to adopt a storytelling format—one that mirrors the cherished moments I spent with my own family. The conversations between Dadaji and Parth serve as a bridge, connecting generations and fostering a sense of curiosity and reverence for our shared heritage. It is my hope that these dialogues will inspire you, just as they inspired me.

This book is designed for modern readers, particularly those taking their first steps into the world of Indian epics. I've endeavored to make the language simple yet evocative, retaining the essence of the *Ramayana* while weaving in contemporary relevance. Each chapter is infused with suspense, philosophy, and vibrant imagery to immerse you in the journey of Rama, Sita, and their companions.

My sincerest gratitude goes to the countless scholars, storytellers, and devotees who have preserved the *Ramayana* through generations. Their work has been a guiding light in my own exploration of this sacred text.

Finally, dear reader, I urge you to approach this book not just as a story but as a mirror—reflecting the values, struggles, and aspirations we all share. May it inspire you to find your own path of righteousness, just as the *Ramayana* continues to illuminate mine.

With humility and hope,
Parth D. Joshi

www.ingramcontent.com/pod-product-compliance
Lightning Source LLC
Chambersburg PA
CBHW021227130726
47988CB00002B/858